A COWGIRL'S DREAM

BARRELS AND HEARTS SERIES BOOK 1

EDITH MACKENZIE

He looked back at Frankie again, a glimmer of respect flickering in his eyes. "I would not ruin her dreams. But maybe she will dream of me too, huh?"

A Cowgirl's Dream (Barrels & Hearts #1):

Images © DepositPhotos – masterwilu & iStock – 4x6

Cover Design © Designed with Grace

❀ Created with Vellum

Thank you, Lexie and Ethan, for letting Mummy write a book.
Nonna, for her kid-wrangling abilities, and Matt for not laughing
in my face when I told him I think I can write a novel.

CHAPTER 1

"Gosh dang it," swore Frankie as she looked down at her horse's front hoof. The shoe clung on precariously, held in place by the two remaining nails. Sighing, she rubbed the gleaming bay on the neck. "It's a good thing you can run fast is all I can say for you, Mac."

Seemingly unfazed, her horse nuzzled her pockets, looking for more licorice. Pushing the strands of long blonde hair that had escaped her braid from her face, she pulled her phone out and sent a quick message to her farrier. Hopefully he would have some spare time soon, and Mac wouldn't be out of work too long.

"Wow, Mac's done it again, hey?" Deb, Frankie's best friend, rested her lanky frame on the fence. "How many has it been this month? Mitch will get the wrong idea," she teased, giving her a suggestive wink.

"You're home early. And I'll have you know—this is only the second time this month." Frankie placed her hands on her hips before laughing. "But to be fair, it was three the month before. And I'm sure Mitch knows Mac's feet have always struggled to hold on to shoes in wet weather. Poor horse isn't a duck, you know."

"Who isn't a duck?" Megan asked, her five-foot frame a stark contrast to Deb's much taller six feet.

"This poor put-upon nag." Frankie glanced between her friends. "Did everyone get an early mark today?" No sooner had the words left her mouth when Mac, offended by the teasing, let out a loud snort, covering the girls in muck. "Friendly." Frankie threw her hands up in mock surrender, causing the girls to laugh harder as Mac stoically returned to looking into the distance, ignoring them.

"Did you get an early knock-off today, too, Deb?" Megan squinted up at her taller friend who nodded in reply.

"Yeah, calm before the storm for us, too. Not long now, and we will be elbow-deep in it for foaling season," Deb answered.

The crunch of the gravel drive drew the girls' attention as a white ute pulled in, its toolbox rattling as if the tools held within sought a way to free themselves. "Here to save the day—and in record time. I want it noted," Mitch said as he emerged, aviator sunglasses glinting in the afternoon sun.

"He can save my day any time he wants," Megan murmured under her breath.

It was true. Mitch, with his sandy-blond hair and chocolate-brown puppy dog eyes, had established quite a following among his clientele. Even the most jaded of pony club mums weren't immune to his boyish charms and had been known to succumb.

Mitch buckled on his farrier chaps—the leather swishing as he strode—carrying his tool stand. "Okay, big boy, let's get this sorted."

The girls appreciatively eyed the farrier's denim-clad butt as he bent to pick up Mac's hoof. With deft movements, he twisted off the remaining nails and inspected the damage to the bent shoe. The girls quickly averted their eyes once he straightened up to avoid being caught staring. Soon, the ring of hammer meeting metal returned the shoe to straight, ready to be reset.

"So, busy day?" *Smooth, gal.* Frankie mentally rolled her eyes at her verbal clumsiness.

"Enough to keep me out of trouble. How about you? Ready for Chaltan Rodeo?"

"Should be, now that you have Mac sorted for me. Are you going down to watch?"

Mitch stretched his back, giving his broad shoulders a wiggle to loosen them. "I'll probably head down for a look. Are all of you riding?"

Megan gave a flick of her hair. "Of course. Gotta keep Frankie honest. If we don't ride against her, she doesn't even try."

Frankie snorted. "I thought it was because of all the cute cowboys."

"Yeah, that too." Deb laughed, winking at Megan.

Reaching into her pocket, Frankie retrieved some cash. "How much do I owe you this time, Mitch?"

"$15 should do it. The rate I'm out here, I'm almost thinking about starting a tab for you." Mitch took a long drink of water, wiping the sweat from his brow. He lingered a moment longer before reluctantly loading his tools into the ute. "If you keep calling me out to tack these shoes back on, I'll expect a dinner invite soon, Frankie," he teased.

"The girl can cook, that's for sure." Deb elbowed Frankie in the side, laughing as Frankie shuffled her feet, her face turning a bright shade of beetroot. "Maybe if you ask her nicely, she will even make dessert for you. That's where she *really* shines."

Mitch visibly brightened at the mention of dessert. "I like sugar."

"I bet he does," whispered Megan.

"Shush." Frankie wanted to disappear in the dirt beneath her feet.

The shrill ring of Mitch's phone saved Frankie from further mortification. "Maybe next time, Frankie," he said, winking at her before climbing into his car and pulling out of the drive.

"Maybe next time," mimicked Deb. "Girl, he has the hots for you."

Megan cast Deb a sour look. "He's just a friendly guy. I don't think he's that into her."

Deb raised her eyebrows, throwing her a frankly disbelieving look, her lips pressed together.

Thankful for a break from being the focus of attention—for the time being, at least—Frankie untied Mac's lead. "Better get evening stables done if we have any hope of getting to that dessert you all keep nattering on about."

There was a chill in the morning air as Frankie made her way to the barn to feed up the horses. The moon still shone pale against an ebony backdrop, its shift nearing completion, and the first hints of color started to paint a thin line on the horizon. Nickers and pawing hooves banged on stable doors, greeting her as she turned on the lights. Mac's brightly shining bay head filled the top of the closest stable door, his big white star glowing. Down the breezeway, the inquisitive eyes of Deb's horse, Doc, peered out at her. Next to him, was the large, spotted head of Megan's horse, Panda. The clamor of clients' horses arose from the remaining stalls, all here to be trained in their owner's fervent hope that some of Frankie's winning magic would rub off on them.

And make no mistake, Frankie was a winner. She just wished people didn't refer to it as luck or magic. She worked danged hard every day to make her dreams come true, and the one she wanted most was to go to the States and qualify for the NFR. If she didn't dare utter to anyone her dream of one day holding the barrel racing gold buckle of the NFR or to be the big winner at the American, then it was solely for fear they would laugh at her.

Finished with the feeding up, she started to change the horses from their warm stable rugs into sturdy green canvas paddock rugs. She enjoyed the steady chomp of contented horses eating and the pungent aromas from the wood shaving bedding wafting up from underfoot. Letting her mind drift, she reflected on the previous night's conversation. Surely Deb had it all wrong about Mitch.

They were friends, and he was a dang good farrier. And if she was being honest with herself, he *was* easy on the eyes. So what if he came running every time she needed him to help with Mac, or always seemed to have a twinkle in his eye when he smiled at her? Still didn't mean he liked her. Surely not in that way, at least. Feeling suddenly hot from the uncomfortable direction her speculations had led her, she began to lead the horses, two at a time, into their paddocks. Time to stop gathering wool and get some real work done.

CHAPTER 2

The rough stock waited in the yards behind the chutes. The anticipation of their upcoming battle against a cowboy made them stamp their feet and hassle each other. Red dust swirled from their maneuvers and was illuminated in the late afternoon sun, giving them a ghoulish appearance. The announcer's scratchy chatter blasted from the loudspeaker, broken up by the crowd's vocal support of the competitors. Frankie always loved the energy that came from being at a rodeo ground. Chalton Rodeo, being their local one, meant they would be able to sleep in their own beds tonight—a welcome change from the usual swag beside the horse trailer.

Frankie gave the cinch one final check before mounting up. Deb and Megan, having already made their runs, cooled their horses down on the other side of the trailer. Walking off on a loose rein, she found some free space in the crowded warm-up area and began to put Mac through his paces. Watching the competitor before her begin to make her way to the entry chute, she completed one final lap before following the other girl's lead. Nerves filtered through her body as the anticipation built. A disappointed roar from the crowd heralded a knocked-down drum.

"And that, ladies and gentlemen, means the cowgirl from Tattergallera is out of the running to bring home a check. And speaking of checks, this little lady about to enter the arena is no stranger to them. Currently leading the championship race to represent Australia at the upcoming Need for Speed competition in the US of A. Make some noise for Frankie Smith."

Wetting her lips, she leaned forward as she gathered up the reins. "Showtime, Mac." She sent him flying down the chute into the arena. Nice and tight around the first drum, the big bay sent sand flying, spraying the closest spectators. She urged him on to the second, and it was neat too.

Now just the last, Mac. Relief flooded her as he left it standing. Sending him flying for home, the wind stung her eyes as he sped to stop the clock. She blinked as she looked up, desperately seeking her time.

15.8 seconds.

"Ladies and gentlemen, our new leader, Frankie Smith, and a brand-new arena record too. Phew, that was one fast run. Put your hands together for our local cowgirl!" Frankie gave Mac a pat, exiting the arena to the crowds' roaring approval.

"Not a bad run for a horse that can't keep his shoes on," observed Mitch. He propped himself nonchalantly against the trailer, hands casually in the pockets of his jeans.

Frankie paused in her task of untacking Mac as she fought the natural inclination to smooth her hair down. *Dang, girl. Settle down.* Feeling rattled, she returned her attention to Mac, painfully aware that her face was red and sweaty from the exertions of her ride. Mitch, in stark contrast, looked like he had stepped straight from a cowgirl's fantasy.

Mac nudged her, looking for treats. Frankie laughed. "He knows he's done a good job, too."

"I'd say you both did a good job." Mitch retrieved a piece of licorice from the packet Frankie always kept in her tack box and gave it to Mac. "So, I think I should buy the new arena record holder a drink," he offered casually, a questioning note in his voice.

"I could go for a drink," Megan said, inviting herself in the conversation as she rounded the corner. "That is, if you're offering."

Mitch, momentarily taken aback, recovered quickly, proving to be too much of a gentleman to correct her. "Sure, my shout for drinks." He shrugged helplessly at Frankie. "Gotta help celebrate your latest win."

And help celebrate he did. Though she wasn't much of a drinker and was also the designated driver, it was one of the best nights Frankie had had in a long time. No one let loose like a rodeo crowd, and tonight they outdid themselves. She allowed Mitch to buy her a small rum and cola and stood back, watching as Deb and Megan kicked up their heels and ran amuck. It was only a matter of time before the hapless Mitch was dragged out to dance.

She laughed at their madcap antics and became aware of the pleading looks Mitch kept throwing her way. Grinning, she put her empty drink down as she prepared to enter the fray. Attempting to save him from her friends' laughing clutches was the least she could do after all the shoes he had tacked back on for her.

It was late by the time Frankie closed the tailgate of the horse trailer after Mitch helped load the horses. Both Deb and Megan snored loudly in the back seat of the ute.

"Um, thank you for helping get the horses sorted. That lot was no help." She gestured to the supine duo. "Oh, and the drink too."

"No problem. I kinda only had you in mind when I offered." He gazed intently at her.

"Um, yeah. Oh, that's what Megan's like, I guess." *Gracious, calm down girl. He's going to think you're a world-class idiot if you keep spluttering about like that.*

"Deb mentioned something about a BBQ you guys are having?"

"Oh yes, for her birthday. She gets one every year." Frankie desperately fought the urge to slap herself on the forehead. *Idiot.*

Mitch laughed. "I hope she gets a birthday every year. Something has gone horribly wrong for her if she doesn't."

Frankie blushed sheepishly. "I meant she has a BBQ every year to celebrate." *Seriously, what was wrong with her?*

"I know what you mean. I was just teasing. Her family always had one for her birthday—I wondered if she'd kept up the tradition. I'd better let you get that lot home." He nodded his head in the direction of the slumbering pair. "I can't wait to try some of these desserts I've heard about at the BBQ."

Why was it that she only owned jeans and T-shirts? Most girls have at least one dress! Giving up, Frankie dramatically flopped face-first onto her bed, deciding she would just spend the entire BBQ in that position. Honestly, there was nothing else she could do.

"Do I even want to know?" Deb popped her head into the room.

"Doff weeve muy loon," she mumbled into the bedspread.

"Duff's a loon? Do we even know a Duff? Hey, Megan, do you know a Duff?" Deb called down the hall.

"No, why?" came the reply from the kitchen.

"Ha-ha, you're so funny," Frankie grumbled, raising her head off the bed. Her hair now closely resembled a bird's nest freshly fallen from a tree. In a storm. A bad one. Maybe cyclonic. "I said Leave. Me. Alone." She theatrically dropped her head back down.

"I'm not sure I can, in clear conscience, remove myself from the room. What sort of friend would I be if I weren't here in your time of"—she helplessly waved her hands in the air—"whatever this is?"

Frankie sighed. "Fine, since you seem to be enjoying this so much, I have nothing to wear."

Deb's mouth twitched a little. "I had noticed you running around naked a lot. I just thought you were trying to even out your tan. Apparently not. Whoa!!" Deb ducked quickly to dodge the pillow Frankie launched at her head. Finding a white shirt Frankie had earlier, she waved it above her head in surrender. "I come in peace. Please, no shoot."

Frankie, despite her peevish mood, couldn't help but laugh. "Fine, but I think I am beyond help."

"My, you *are* committing to drama today, aren't you? Is it because the farrier stud muffin is coming over?"

Frankie snorted in an unladylike manner. "Dare you to call him that to his face."

"I would, but I want him to be able to fit his hat back on his head at some point," Deb deadpanned. "Okay, let's have a look at what we're working with here." She headed confidently to Frankie's closet.

In the end, Frankie did find something to wear, and it was jeans and a shirt. But hey, Deb had to work with what she had. Her long blonde hair hung sleekly from a high ponytail and her jeans hugged her slender curves, the lean muscles shaped from long hours in the saddle. The merle-grey V-neck T-shirt clung just enough in the right places. Deb didn't care what Frankie thought. She was pretty sure Mitch wasn't going to have any complaints.

CHAPTER 3

*D*eb may have unkindly called Frankie a coward for saying only a quick hello to Mitch before bolting off to the kitchen to finish preparing dessert. Quite a crowd had gathered for Deb's annual birthday BBQ, which wasn't unusual with the rodeo community since they could so easily go from competitors to friends to family. Placing the final scoop of passionfruit on the pavlova, she rubbed her nose as she stepped back to appreciate her masterpiece.

"I was starting to think you might be avoiding me. But now I see what you've been up to, I fully support you hiding out," Mitch said from the doorway.

Frankie grinned. "Behold, my masterful confectionary treat that I like to call *Frankie's Fab Pav*."

Frankie's breath caught as Mitch advanced, his eyes focused on her … nose? *Why the heck was he staring at her nose?* Instinctively, she lifted her hand just as he reached forward. For the briefest of moments, their hands touched. Feeling flustered, Frankie dropped her eyes quickly, her cheeks growing hot as he brushed a finger gently over the tip of her nose.

"You have some passionfruit juice on your nose," he said, suppressed laughter clear in his voice. Her eyes were riveted to his mouth. She watched as he slowly sucked the liquid off his fingers. "Yep, definitely passionfruit."

She blushed harder, feeling foolish for having thought he might have been on the verge of making a move on her. Vexed, she fought the urge to fan herself. "I'm always a hot mess in the kitchen."

Mitch still hadn't moved back. His proximity made the butterflies in her stomach do backflips. "I like the hot-mess Frankie. She's kinda cute." He brushed a stray strand of hair away from her face.

Her mouth went dry and all power of speech deserted her. *Did he just do that? Calm down, gal, and say something witty*! Before she could formulate a response, he leaned in and kissed her gently on the lips.

As he stepped back, she said the only thing she could manage. "Huh."

Mitch rubbed the back of his neck. "Good huh, or bad huh?"

Eyes wide, she broke out into a grin. "I would definitely say a good huh."

"Everyone will think you two are hiding out in here," Megan huffed, bustling into the room. She stopped, her eyes narrowing suspiciously. "Did I interrupt something?"

"Wouldn't be the first," Mitch muttered under his breath.

Megan tilted her head questioningly. "Sorry, what?"

"Just that she has made a spectacular dessert," he pronounced more clearly, not taking his eyes off Frankie. "I better head back. I'm not very good around temptation." He gave Frankie a conspiratorial wink.

Megan leveled both of them a hard look before hooking her arm through Mitch's, leaving Frankie alone to gather the remnants of her scattered wits.

~

The fire crackled, sending sparks floating up into the clear night sky. The stars were brilliant in the distance. A few strains of Miranda Lambert drifted toward Frankie, conversation swirling around her. Feeling her thoughts drifting to the events that had transpired in the kitchen, she pulled herself back to the present. She took a sip of her drink, feeling, rather than seeing, the sharp glare being directed at her. Looking around curiously, it surprised her to see Megan on the other end of it.

Gosh, what now? She sighed. *It's not like I don't have other things to stress about.*

Deb waved from the other side of the fire, getting her attention. "Did you hear, Frankie? About Cassie?"

Focusing on her, Frankie leaned forward in her camp chair. "Sorry. What about Cassie?"

"Her and James are having a baby."

Frankie turned toward the couple beside Deb. "Congratulations you guys! How far along?"

"Just out of the first trimester. That's actually why I had to cancel going to my last rodeo. It was still too early to tell anyone, but you were an absolute godsend helping look after my stepson while I tried to act like I didn't want to throw up everywhere. You'd make a great mum, Frankie. You just need to find the right guy."

Frankie's smile froze on her lips. "Um, yeah. I definitely want kids. But you know, the right time and all that."

She returned to sipping her drink, desperately hoping that would be the end of that line of conversation. Feeling awkward, her gaze bounced around the faces by the fire before landing on Mitch. His expression was unfathomable as he returned her look.

As the evening drew to a close, Frankie was surprised Mitch had made no further attempts to engage her in conversation. A sick feeling began to gather in her stomach as she tried not to overthink it. Maybe he just wanted to play it cool while everyone was around. Maybe he wanted to take it slow.

As Mitch stood and began to make his excuses to leave, Frankie's feelings of insecurity increased. She joined her friends as they escorted him to his car before bidding him farewell. Frankie desperately tried to find a reason to get her friends to leave her alone with Mitch. But none of her subtle hints worked, and she was forced to simply wave goodnight and watch him drive off. Mitch had given no hints that he even remembered kissing her in the kitchen, and she began to wonder if maybe she'd imagined it all.

Later that night, she curled up in bed, staring at her phone. She didn't know if she should send him a message or play the waiting game and leave it alone. She suspected that she might very well go insane while she waited. It was hard not to run through the kiss again and again in her mind, trying to understand what, exactly, had changed after it. Giving an exasperated sigh, she put the pillow over her head and attempted to sleep.

"I'm sorry he did *what?*" screeched Deb. "Back up, I want minute details. Megan, get your butt in here!"

Deb waited impatiently as Megan made her way groggily into the kitchen. Frankie could sympathize. This morning, she felt like a befuddled pigeon that had fallen headfirst from its nest. A miserable night's sleep would do that to a girl.

"Can I at least pour myself a coffee before you bombard me?" Megan grumbled. Deb waved her over to the kettle.

"Okay, from the beginning. Don't spare any details." Deb propped herself up on the kitchen bench.

"This had better be worth it." Megan took a cautious sip of her brew.

"Um, so last night, Mitch kissed me."

"What? When?" Enlightenment dawned on Megan's face before it hardened. "It was in the kitchen, right? When I walked in on you two together?" Frankie's eyes narrowed suspiciously. If she didn't know better, she would have said her friend sounded jealous.

"How was it?" Deb asked, leaning forward on her elbows. "Was he any good?"

"Yeah. I mean, I think so? I don't really have much else to compare it to," Frankie stammered, blushing.

"Well, from what I hear, he has lots of practice," Megan added sourly.

"Well, it doesn't matter anyway," Frankie said, lifting her chin defiantly. "I must have done something wrong, because he didn't seem to want anything more to do with me after it." Tears threatened to spill as her tough façade began to crumble.

Megan gave a sad smile. "Aww, hun, I'm sorry."

Deb looked at her suspiciously before returning her attention back to Frankie. "I'm sure you did nothing wrong. Maybe he just got distracted at the party."

"Yeah, right. He kissed me and then got busy being social. Somehow, that doesn't seem believable." Frankie was doubtful. Shifting gears, she looked at Megan intently. "And while I'm at it, why have you been so weird lately?"

"Our little Megan has a bit of a crush on Mitch," Deb said smugly. "Has since we first met him in kindergarten. I think she's jealous of the attention you're getting."

Megan's cheeks grew red and she shifted in her chair. "Fine," she huffed. "I think he's hot. But after how he's acting toward Frankie, he's a jerk. Anyway, he was your best friend in kindy, not mine."

"He is a jerk." Frankie sniffled. "I just feel like such an

idiot. Why are men like that?" she cried bitterly. Megan and Deb wrapped her up tight in a group hug. For a moment, love surrounded her. Her resolve strengthened. "I'll be fine. You know what? I'll be better than fine. I'm gonna train and work until I get my dreams. I will become the gosh dang world champ and to bloody heck with men!"

CHAPTER 4

*T*he sweet smell of molasses and hay mingled with the headier musk of horse sweat as coats gleamed and muscles rippled. The steady drum of hoofbeats provided the soundtrack to the days that followed. And keeping time with it was the constant chant—*world champ, world champ*. Frankie was determined that nothing would get in her way, especially a man. Tamboro was the final rodeo for the year. If she could keep momentum and finish in the top three, she could win herself a ticket to the Need for Speed finals in Fort Worth, Texas. Easy.

Tamboro was a three-hour drive from home, and the girls set off at sparrow's fart—bright and early. They hoped to give their horses time to settle in and a chance to recover from the drive. Mac stood, his burnished mahogany bay coat glistening in the sun, the defined muscles underneath giving the impression of barely-contained power. As she brushed him, it was clear all her work hadn't been for naught. Now all Frankie had to do was get her mind back in the game and not get rattled by anything or, should she say, anyone. Both Deb and Megan had assured her they would run interference if Mitch should come anywhere near her before her race.

"Earth to champ?"

Frankie looked up to see Megan and Deb looking at her. "Sorry, what?"

"Deb and I were just going to head on over to the registration tent and get signed in. You about done there and wanna come?" Megan said.

"Yeah, you know, safety in numbers?" Deb added.

Frankie placed her brush back in her tack box and shut the lid, picking it up. She stowed it in the trailer. "Yeah, I guess so."

Deb gave her a sympathetic smile and put an arm around her shoulders. Frankie wasn't sure if she did it as a show of support or to stop her from bolting at the first sign of trouble. She chose to believe it was the former as Megan fell into step beside them. The short walk to sign in was thankfully uneventful. The friends greeted the handful of people they passed on their way, and the tent was empty upon their arrival.

"Easy peasy," Deb said as they started walking back. Frankie gave her a weak smile and jammed her hands in her pockets.

"Yeah," said Megan. "That's the hard bit taken care of. All you need to do now is place tonight." She gave Frankie a cheery wink.

"Sure thing. Easy as, mate." Frankie laughed. Her friends, at last, were lifting her spirits.

"Bugger, keep walking," Megan muttered.

"What?" Frankie looked around them as Deb frog-marched her as fast as she could. "Guys, what the heck?"

"It's Mitch!" Megan hissed.

With a sinking feeling, Frankie finally located him. He was engaged in an animated conversation with one of the stock contractors, throwing his head back as he laughed. Cold, hard anger coursed through her body at the sight of him. Before she could analyze her feelings, her feet were already in locomotion, her steps rapidly eating up the distance between them.

"Crap," Deb said from behind her.

"What the bloody heck do we do now?" Megan looked to her tall friend for guidance.

"Casually loiter, I guess."

Mitch had just finished his conversation when she bore down on him. He seemed startled by her sudden appearance, though her slightly deranged expression might have had something to do with that.

"Hey, Frankie. How have you been?" His voice was slightly strained.

"Well, Mitch, thank you for asking," she snapped. Mitch cringed at her tone. "I've been working on my mental toughness."

"That's—"

Frankie held her hand up to silence him. "Oh, hun. I'm not finished yet. You see, some jerk kissed me and then has ghosted me ever since. Pretty crap timing if you ask me, what with everything riding on this rodeo tonight. Head games and all that. Lord knows I couldn't think straight when he was around. What an idiot he must have thought I was."

"Frankie, I'm—"

"Still not finished," she ground out. "Turns out I'm pretty tough. So, you want to tell me why you are all over me like a rash and then drop me like a lead balloon the next minute? Did I completely misread the situation?"

"You didn't misread it. I liked you." Mitch sighed and rubbed his hand through his hair. "I like you," he corrected himself.

"You have a strange way of showing it."

Mitch stared at the ground uncomfortably before finally finding the nerve to look back up and stare into her eyes. "I didn't know you wanted kids."

Frankie's mouth dropped open. "What? Yeah, like, eventually. One day. Far down the track." She stressed the word *far*. "Not now."

"It doesn't matter when you want them. I can't have them."

She blinked rapidly. "Um, okay. Don't you think you're getting a little ahead of yourself there? I mean, we only kissed."

Mitch gave a sad little smile. "Yeah, but I know you, Frankie. You're loyal. And if I'd let things keep going, and then you found out, you would have been committed and that isn't fair. And I don't know if I could have let you go, even if that meant knowing that one day you would hate me for not being able to give you kids."

Frankie swallowed. "I—I don't really know what to say. I think you're a coward and should have let me have a say. You ran away and made me feel like it was me." She shook her head slowly. "I need to get ready."

Without another word, she spun on her heels and headed back toward Deb and Megan. Her friends appeared to be doing their level best to classify the type of gravel they were standing on.

"Frankie, I'm sorry," called Mitch.

"So am I."

Frankie smoothed down her black and teal arena shirt, her heart accelerating as she entered the chute. *Three drums, gal. That's all you need to keep standing. Three drums.* Mac began to tense underneath her, his footfalls quickening as he waited for her to give him his cue to go. She gathered up her reins and nudged her legs.

Mac sprung forward, finally released to run. They cleared the first drum before the commentator even introduced them. Then, just like that, the second drum was completed, and Mac's ears pricked forward, his attention focused on the task before him. The crowd roared their approval as they rounded the third drum and flew to the finish line. The outside world slowly crept back into Frankie's consciousness.

"Ladies and gentlemen, put your hands together for this year's Australian Need for Speed Champion, Frankie Smith. This little lady has booked herself a ticket to represent Australia at the world event in Texas, and maybe even a chance to earn her Pro Card."

"You did it!" Megan squealed as Deb almost pulled Frankie off Mac to give her a giant hug. Mac danced on the spot, the blood still coursing through his veins.

"I can't believe it! I mean, I believe you did it!" Deb hollered, jumping up and down.

Slowly, as the adrenaline left her body, Frankie felt curiously numb. It was as if all the pent-up stress drained from her overwrought muscles, leaving them feeling like liquid. There was still a great deal to organize—travel, a lease horse, and somewhere to train in the States. But for now, all she wanted to do was soak in the moment with her friends.

CHAPTER 5

*I*f Frankie had thought that things would calm down after she qualified, she was sadly mistaken. The local newspaper called to interview her, as did the local news. She still hadn't found a barn to base herself, or a horse to lease for the event. And it wasn't as simple as finding just any equine partner either. The horse had to be well-trained and competing at a high level for her to have any chance at all.

"How's the search going?" asked Megan after returning from work to find Frankie hunched at her laptop in despair. Again.

"I feel like a clock is ticking, and every day I can't find a horse, the more I think of all this effort to qualify, and for what if I don't find one?" Frankie slammed the laptop shut in frustration. "I give up." She put her face down on the offensive device in defeat. "Well, not really. That was more for a dramatic effect."

"I might have something that may be worth following up on."

Frankie's head perked up. "I'm listening."

"One owner whose yearling I prepped last year—

Hernando? You remember me talking about him? Little Brazilian guy? He made his money in waxing?"

"I think so."

"Well, I was telling him about your current predicament, and he thinks he might be able to help or at least put you in touch with someone that can help. He has a niece that lives just out of Fort Worth in a place called Benbrook, and she apparently has just started out breeding barrel horses."

"I don't exactly have time for foals to grow up," Frankie stated.

"Yes, but she has bought a nice barrel horse. Hernando said that she planned on getting her campaigned for the next few years before retiring her to the broodmare paddock."

"Interesting," Frankie said.

"I thought so." Megan tossed a scrap of paper on the desk. "Anyway, these are her details if you want to contact her. What have you got to lose?"

It turned out that Gabriella, or 'Everyone just calls me Gabi', was more than willing to help. She'd offered an opportunity to try the mare and, if suitable, to lease her for the six weeks prior to and including the Need for Speed World Championship. To top it off, she had a spare room in the bunkhouse of her family's ranch that she was happy for Frankie to base out of. When Frankie thanked her profusely, she simply informed her that, although she was delighted to help her, she was first and foremost a businesswoman. And a good enough one to recognize it wouldn't hurt her stud to have a horse running at the event.

"Are you ready?" Deb asked.

Frankie leaned against the top rail of the fence, rubbing Mac's neck as he nosed her for more treats. "What happens if I'm not?"

"I'd have to give you a thrashing. Now, I suggest you get your arse into gear, so you don't miss this flight."

"No, I mean, what if I'm not ready for over there? Then what?"

"Then you'll do what you always do. You'll train harder, smarter, and you will make yourself good enough. You will go over there and show them what an Aussie chick can do around those cans."

Frankie smiled. "Thanks. I needed to hear that."

"Actually, I got most of that from Doctor Phil." Deb chuckled. Frankie gave her a light punch to the shoulder that made her laugh even harder.

"What am I going to do without you guys over there?"

"Probably become a champ." Deb's face became serious. "I mean that, Frankie. You are an incredible horsewoman. You got this, and we will be there for the finals anyway."

Frankie's throat tightened, and she swallowed against the emotion building. "I guess I had better grab that suitcase so we can go."

Deb doffed a mock hat in her direction, "Your chauffeur will wait in the car."

Twenty-four hours later, Frankie finally made it to Fort Worth, or as she liked to call it, escaped the clutches of international travel. Crammed into economy, her discomfort had escalated from numb bum or, as she coined it, Numbus Bumus to pain, or Arsus Hurtus. Walking out of customs, she scanned the crowd, her heart racing anxiously for someone to be there to pick her up. A sea of signs bombarded the arriving passengers and were overwhelming in their sheer volume. She felt light-headed from relief when she eventually located her name. She looked into an open, friendly face. "Gabi?"

"Frankie, I am so glad to finally meet you. Was the flight good?" The attractive, young dark-haired woman asked warmly.

"It was good, but I am so glad to be off a plane at last."

"I bet. Shall we get going and I can show you your casa while you are here?" Gabi smiled sympathetically.

"That would be great."

Gabi led the way outside of the airport to a large Dodge truck and helped lift Frankie's bag into the back. A slight kerfuffle followed with Frankie attempting to hop in the passenger side, only to find it was the driver's side. Once it was sorted, it didn't take long for them to hit traffic and head out of town.

I have to remember the cars are back to front here, she thought as she settled back into her seat.

It was nearly dark by the time they pulled into a long gravel drive. At the entrance was a large wooden slab which had *Rancho do Paraiso do Cavalerio do Touro* branded onto it. Frankie looked at it curiously, her Portuguese almost non-existent. Noticing her confused look, Gabi laughed.

"My father was one of the first Brazilian bull riders to make it big in the States. When my parents first came here, they had nothing, and he was so proud he could buy this place from his winnings. He still helps any of the Brazilian riders that come over, helps with learning English, some-where to stay, guidance on tour. Pretty much anything they need. One day, one of the guys, Luciano, said my father had created a bull rider's paradise, and so he decided to name the ranch that. Personally, I'm hoping to add my mark that says Affinity Ranch Stud, home to barrel horse champions." Her hands gestured as if it was spelled in lights.

"Let's see what we can do about starting with home to Need for Speed World Champion," Frankie offered.

"I like the sound of that."

The ranch building appeared at the end of the drive, a

warm, welcoming glow coming from the windows of the house. Frankie could make out a large barn and machinery shed to the other side of it.

"Home, sweet home." Gabi gave a welcoming flourish.

"What is it in Portuguese?" Frankie glanced at the Brazilian woman.

"Lar doce lar."

"Lar doce lar," Frankie repeated as she climbed down from the car, stretching her fatigued muscles.

The front screen door opened, and an older, rather distinguished, silver-haired gentleman appeared. He had a robust and open face. Frankie immediately saw the resemblance to the Brazilian girl.

"Papai," greeted Gabi. "This is Frankie. Frankie, this is my father, Eduardo."

Eduardo walked forward. "Hello, Frankie, I am pleased to finally meet you." He pulled her into a warm embrace. "My wife is inside just finishing up dinner. If you like, I will take your bag to your room."

"Thank you, Senhor Eduardo, that would be great."

"Papai, remember what we spoke about. She is staying in the spare room in the bunkhouse with me," warned Gabi.

A flurry of Portuguese flew between father and daughter in what seemed to Frankie to be quite an animated fashion. With one final grudging look to his daughter, he picked up Frankie's suitcase and headed to the barn.

"Forgive my father. He can sometimes be a little old-fashioned. You have no idea how long it took for him to come around when I moved out of the house all the way over to the barn." Gabi laughed at the memory. "Mae and Papai both think it is more suitable for you to stay in the house, but you are here as my guest. So, I win."

"Remind me not to go against you." Frankie admired Gabi's moxie.

"I try to be on the winning side. But then again, I come

from a *very* competitive family. I think I smell Feijoada cooking."

"I'm not sure I have ever had that before," said Frankie, her stomach grumbling loudly. The noise continued as if in protest, reminding her that all she had had for the last twenty-four hours was airplane food.

"You are in for a real treat. It's like, the classic Brazilian dish, and my mom just so happens to make a mean version of it." The two girls stepped off the porch and into the house in comfortable companionship, both eager to lay waste to the meal inside.

Much later, after saying her goodnights to the family, Frankie lay snugly in her room in the bunkhouse, her belly comfortably full. The Cabrera family had included her as if she was a long-lost family member, their warm hospitality a balm to her jangled nerves of being in a strange environment. She closed her eyes tightly against the pressure she felt building, the anxiety rising in a wave. Breathing deeply, she pulled the covers tightly up under her chin as if it was protective armor. Lost in a cloud of warmth and shattered exhaustion, she drifted off to sleep.

CHAPTER 6

"This is Delila." Gabi proudly led the buckskin mare out of her stall. "The pride of Affinity Ranch Stud."

Frankie looked the mare over curiously, liking what she saw in front of her. Delila was the color of fresh-from-the-oven biscuits, of which Frankie had just that morning been introduced to at breakfast. She couldn't wait to tell her friends back home that biscuits, cookies and scones were all messed about in America. Returning her attention to the mare, she admired the horse's legs that finished in a glossy black, perfectly matched by her silky ebony mane and tail. To Frankie's experienced eye, she was a well-put-together and strong looking mare. This would work just fine.

"She's nice. Really nice," Frankie said appreciatively, her hand stroking the velvety muzzle that reached out to sniff her.

"Well, let's get her saddled up, and you can see what she can do. I guess at the same time, I can see what you can do, too."

"No pressure at all." Frankie's eyes twinkled in antic-ipation.

"None. But you doing well with my mare could put my

breeding program on the map." Gabi, her eyes solemn, stared out across the paddocks.

"Well, you've got one heck of a start with this mare. Now, which saddle is hers?" Frankie said.

Despite her confident exterior, inside, the nerves began to flutter, dancing like a kite in a storm. Delila quickly put any doubts to rest. Frankie couldn't quite believe her luck to have secured the ride on such a well-trained, talented barrel horse. She whooped in delight as she completed the pattern, patting the prancing Delila enthusiastically.

"Good girl. You know you're a champion, don't you?" she crooned. For the first time, she dared to hope that maybe, with Delila, she might just have a chance. Completing her cooling down, she walked her mount to where Gabi perched on the rails with her father beside her.

Gabi wore a relieved smile. "I have watched the videos of your rides, but in the flesh, you are even more of an extraordinary horsewoman. I think the two of you are a good match."

Frankie blushed happily as she wiped the sweat from her brow. "Thanks for trusting me with your mare, it means a lot."

"Papai has just reminded me we are having a churrasco in your honor this evening. He has invited some people over."

"What is a churrasco?" Frankie asked curiously, not entirely sure what she was getting into.

"It is a gathering. We eat, drink, talk important affairs." Senhor Eduardo's merry smile was infectious. "In this case, show off our Australian guest."

Frankie was again beginning to feel an all-too-familiar sense of panic rise up. It must have shown on her face because Gabi looked alarmed. "Are you okay?"

"But I don't have anything to wear!"

∼

The sweet woody char of smoky meat and other aromas Frankie couldn't quite identify wafted through the open window of her bedroom. Gabi was laying out every piece of clothing Frankie had brought with her on the bed, her lips pursed as she made little murmurings under her breath. Judging from the way she discarded each item almost as soon as she had picked it up, Frankie suspected she didn't entirely approve of her dress sense. It didn't help in the slightest that Frankie didn't have the foggiest idea what to wear to a churrasco. Giving up, Gabi threw her hands up in the air, muttered something in Portuguese that Frankie suspected was not entirely polite and left the room.

Frankie flopped down in stunned silence, not sure what she should do. Tears threatened as homesickness overwhelmed her. She began to sniffle, missing Deb and Megan. Before she could completely surrender to self-pity, Gabi popped back into the room. She carried a white lace dress in one hand and a pair of boots in the other.

"I think we are close in size. Let's try these on."

The dress had floating white sleeves and finished just above the knee. It fit just as if it had been made for her. She seated herself on the bed and began to pull a boot on. Her foot hit something cold inside it. Giving a shriek, she jumped to her feet, frantically trying to flick the boot off. Gabi doubled with laughter.

"I don't know why you are laughing! There's something in there!" she said indignantly.

Wiping tears of mirth away, Gabi pulled out a turquoise necklace and matching belt. "I am so sorry, Frankie. I forgot to mention that I put these in here because I ran out of hands to carry everything. You should have seen your face and that noise you made…" Once again, her body shook with laughter.

Frankie's lips began to twitch. "I thought it was a bloody cane toad."

"What's a cane toad?"

"Ugly, warty, poisonous pest toad. They like to hide in any shoes you leave about outside." She looked down at the boots. They were a beautiful dark tan color with tooled roses that had been colored black. She had never seen a pair as beautiful back home. "These are gorgeous."

"They are, but I hardly wear them. They pinch my feet. If you like them, you can have them."

Frankie pulled them on, experimentally standing up and taking a few steps. "They feel great."

"Good, now for the finishing touches. Come over here." Gabi cinched in her waist with the turquoise belt and draped the necklace around her neck. The squash blossom design finished at her breastbone. The Brazilian girl began to fuss with her hair. "I wish I could get my hair to this shade." She gestured at Frankie's honey-blonde locks. "Now, sit while I do something with this."

Frankie sat obediently. "Work your magic."

To be fair, in her time, Frankie had been to too many BBQ's. Nothing prepared her for a churrasco. The tables groaned under what appeared to be an endless supply of beef, smoky chicken wings, buttery garlic bread, squeaky cheese, and pork sausages. Her stomach groaned a grumbling gurgle.

Gabi laughed. "I think you have a good appetite. Do you want caipirinhas? Or would you prefer a beer?"

"What is a caipirinha?"

"It's a cocktail made with Cachaca, lime and sugar. I have to warn you, if you aren't used to them, they can be lethal," Gabi stressed.

"She'll be right. If there's one thing that Aussies can do, it's hold their booze," Frankie boasted, careful to omit that this particular Aussie didn't quite fit the stereotype.

"Booze?"

"Grog, booze, piss. You know, alcohol. Anyway, that drink sounds great, I'll try one."

As Gabi walked off to find some drinks, Frankie self-consciously moved to one side of the food table. Curiously, she looked around at the various groups of people gathered. She found herself on the other end of a gaze with frankly the most magnetically attractive man she had ever laid eyes on. The stranger had the swarthy complexion of most of the assembled guests. He gave a slow, seductive smile while he returned her candid appraisal, a hot-blooded gleam flaring in his dark, smiling eyes, the corners crinkling into lines that looked well-used. The man had a smile that would put a Hollywood actor to shame.

"Here you go. I should warn you—"

Before Gabi could finish, Frankie took the drink from her and drained it. Her regret was almost immediate. No sooner had the fluid hit the back of her throat when it induced an extreme burning sensation. Frankie could only imagine it was how a marshmallow felt just before it turned into a blistered, gooey mess on the fire. At this stage, she wasn't even sure her esophagus still existed, let alone functioned as she vigorously exploded into a coughing fit.

Gabi pounded her on the back while snorting with merriment. Finally, her ability to inhale oxygen was restored, and she wiped away the tears her misadventure had caused her to shed.

"I tried to warn you." Gabi said between bouts of laughter.

"I know, but surely some sympathy is in order here?"

"None." Gabi drew in a deep, steadying breath, attempting to subdue her laughter. "Oh, I forgot, Papai wants us to come over and say hi to some people. Apparently, Luciano really wants to meet you."

Frankie followed Gabi, aware of a pleasant languidness settling over her now that the burning had subsided from the caipirinhas. Senhor Eduardo was deep in conversation with a couple of men. Hollywood Smile from earlier was sipping a beer while he listened. Upon their arrival, the conversation ceased.

"Ah, girls, I have some people here that I would like to introduce Frankie too. Frankie this is Joao Rojas." He gestured with his drink to a dark-haired man who appeared to be in his twenties. Joao nodded politely. He had the softest, kindest eyes Frankie had ever seen outside of a Labrador puppy. "And this, Frankie, is Luciano Navarro." He placed an arm around Hollywood Smile. "Both are making Brazil proud as bull riders on the PBR."

Luciano stepped forward, beaming his megawatt smile, the air around him crackling with vitality as he extended a hand to Frankie. "Ola, Frankie. Eduardo had not told us that Gabriella's amiga was so bonita."

Finding herself on the receiving end of such pure maleness, warmth flowed up into Frankie's face, infusing it a bright scarlet. She desperately prayed it was too dark for Luciano to be able to tell. She had no idea what he had called her, but the intimate tone left her feeling flustered.

"Leave her alone, Luciano." Gabi stepped between them, wagging her finger in warning. "Frankie is not some buckle bunny plaything. She is here to chase a dream just like you, so don't mess it up for her."

He looked back at Frankie again, a glimmer of respect flickering in his eyes. "I would not ruin her dreams. But maybe she will dream of me too, huh?"

He gave a shrug of his broad shoulders. Frankie stood riveted, never having been the recipient of such a directly amorous look, a tingle beginning in her belly.

"I doubt there is room in my dreams for such a big ego." She smiled sweetly. Joao and Senhor Eduardo snickered. "Joao, it was nice to meet you. Maybe next time, this one here"—she pointed at Luciano—"won't hog all the attention."

With a saucy wink, she flounced off with Gabi beside her chuckling.

"I am so glad I didn't miss that. Luciano usually has the ladies fall in a heap at his feet. Did you see his face?" Gabi giggled at the memory.

"No, I was too busy making a dramatic exit. I figured amiga means friend, but what does bonita mean?"

"Our Luciano thinks you are beautiful." Gabi waggled her eyebrows comically.

For what felt like the hundredth time that evening, Frankie blushed. "Well, he can think that all he wants. But after the last one, give me horses anytime. At least then, the only males I have to deal with are nice, quiet geldings!"

CHAPTER 7

*T*he next few weeks flew by in a flurry of time spent with Delila, getting to know her quirks, and helping around the ranch with various tasks. It hadn't taken Frankie long to notice the black colt that only Senhor Eduardo handled. As she performed her jobs about the ranch throughout the day, she always found herself drawn back to the colt. Fixated on the horse, she was determined to discover his story and why such a magnificent creature was largely ignored.

"Senhor Eduardo, that black colt of yours is something else." Frankie admired the horse. "He can jump into my suitcase anytime he wants."

Senhor Eduardo looked sadly at the colt playfully splashing his muzzle into the water trough. The water droplets caught the sun as they flicked through the air. "I had high hopes for him. With his bloodlines, he should be a champion, but no one can handle him long enough to even break him. He is just too unpredictable. That is why I will not let Gabriella handle him." Senhor Eduardo sighed heavily. "It is a shame, especially with Gabriella trying to breed champions. I guess he will not be one of them."

Frankie's eyes narrowed with a determined glint. "What's his name?"

The older man gave her a steady look. "We have never named him as nothing seemed to stick. He was always an odd one."

Frankie frowned. "It seems a shame to me. I've worked with some tricky ones back home. Maybe I could give it a shot," she offered, holding her breath hopefully.

Senhor Eduardo clasped Frankie on the shoulder and gave it a gentle squeeze. "You have not been here long, Frankie, but I will say to you what I say to my own daughter. No man can trust that horse, and I won't allow you to get hurt trying." He smiled sadly. "I say that not to be mean, but I do not want anything to happen to you." He let his hand drop. "Now, if I remember correctly, are you not collecting your friends today?"

Frankie bounced excitedly off the fence. "Sure am. Thank you so much for letting them stay here. It's going to be awesome having my Aussie support team here for the last week leading up to Need for Speed."

"Your family is my family, Frankie," he said magnanimously. "Now, off you go."

As she walked off, Frankie couldn't resist one last glance over her shoulder. The colt had now ambled off and was pawing at the ground, the dust rising about him in a cloud. With a grunt, he lowered himself and began to roll enthusiastically, kicking his legs in the air. After easing all of his various itches, he hauled himself back to his feet, shaking the dirt from his coat.

Maybe Senhor Eduardo is right, she thought. *No man can trust him. But he didn't say anything about a woman!*

Frankie gave a little squeal of excitement as Deb and Megan

made their way through the crowded arrivals lounge. The girls ran toward each other, colliding in a big and long-overdue group hug. Now, as Frankie cautiously pulled into the driveway, she was surprised to see several trucks parked up.

"Thank bloody heck we survived that!" Deb threw a hand dramatically to her forehead. "I think this Gabi chick is pretty brave letting you drive her truck."

"Hey, it wasn't that bad."

"Ah, you drifted into oncoming traffic," Megan pointed out.

"Once. I did that once. If you guys are such experts, one of you can drive next time. It's not as easy doing everything in reverse as you might think," Frankie protested.

"Personally, my favorite was how many times you put the windscreen wipers on when you wanted to indicate," Deb teased.

"Are you finished?" Frankie opened her palms toward them.

"Oh, my. Who are they?" Megan asked in breathless admiration, looking to the porch.

Frankie turned, suspicion already forming in her mind. As she had suspected, standing with one lean snugly-clad denim hip against the porch rail, beer in his hand, was Luciano. He glanced at Frankie, sending her his signature cocky Hollywood smile before returning to his conversation with Joao and Senhor Eduardo.

"The older silver-haired gentleman is Gabi's dad, Senhor Eduardo. The other two are some bull riders he knows," she said dismissively.

"I would like to get to know them, too," said Deb, enjoying the view. She threw her arms around Megan and Frankie's shoulders as they headed to the barn. "I think I'm going to like it here."

After introducing the girls to Gabi, Frankie left them to

settle in and unpack while she went down to check up on Delila. She found the buckskin mare munching on a hay net in her stall. She gave a little nicker of recognition before returning back to her hay. Walking further down the barn, her feet led her to the last stall. Inside, the dark colt had pulled his hay out and was flicking it through the air. Frankie pulled an apple from her pocket.

"Hey, big boy," she called softly as he eyed her curiously.

"I had hoped you were talking to me," Luciano said from behind her.

She jumped in surprise, causing the colt to give a startled snort and take a step back. Sighing in frustration, Frankie placed the apple on top of the stall door before turning around, her hands on her hips.

"Do you make a habit of sneaking up on girls in barns?" she asked tartly.

"Not so much sneaking up on girls in barns. But yes, much experience with girls, sneaking, and barns." His smile was smug, and he shrugged his broad shoulders. He offered her one of the beers he was holding. "Have a drink with me."

For a moment, Frankie was dazzled by his powerful presence and forgot to breathe. Shaking the thoughts from her mind, she took the proffered beer. "Sure. Does Senhor Eduardo know you are lurking about his barn?"

"I used to live in the bunkhouse when I first moved here. Joao and I bunked together. That was when Gabriella still lived in the house, unfortunately for Joao."

Frankie looked at Luciano in surprise, her eyes sparkling with interest. "Joao has a thing for Gabi?"

"Yes. He can ride tough bulls, but scared of talking to a girl." Luciano shook his head in mock despair. "This I do not understand."

"I can imagine." Frankie took a sip of her beer. "Did you find it hard to settle into the tour?"

"Very tough." Frankie was surprised by his candor. "I

spoke no English, did not know how things work here. Senhor Eduardo helps all of us that come over. When he came, there was no one."

"He seems like a nice guy."

"What do you think about me?"

Frankie spluttered on her beer, succumbing to a coughing fit as she attempted to breathe.

"Frankie, are you not used to the liquor? I recall you having trouble drinking at the churrasco." Luciano's face was a picture of concern.

"I can handle it just fine, I'll have you know," she snapped. "It's just that, well, that was very direct."

"Is that not best? I would know what you think about me." He gave her his best sexy smirk.

Frankie made a show of giving him the once over. His jeans hung about his slim hips, the denim encasing a butt that was definitely perv-worthy. The V-neck T-shirt he wore was tight enough to make out the definition of his muscles and Frankie strongly suspected there was a six-pack hidden underneath. His biceps were defined, mute evidence of working on a ranch and riding bulls for a living.

Frankie was momentarily distracted by the whisper of a thought that entered her head. *What would it be like to be held by those arms?* She skirted around the image that forced its way into her mind, fighting against the desire to succumb to the darkly compelling thought. His body was rugged, and power and confidence emanated from him. But it was his face that Frankie found herself dangerously affected by. It was the sheer force of his personality that made it so darkly magnetic. The strength of his character animatedly shone from his dark, gleaming eyes. Eyes that were currently fixed warmly on her.

His sensuous lips drew back into his now familiar smile, and Frankie recognized herself being drawn in by his charm, aware of just how easy it would be to get entangled in it. She had an inkling that, just like a fly stuck in the spider's web, most women probably only realized when it was too late to escape. Or maybe they didn't want to escape after a while. She shook her head to clear her mind of that particular notion.

Frankie hesitated. "I think you are a handsome man who knows he is a handsome man."

"So, you like me," he stated confidently. He folded his arms over his chest, pulling his shirt tighter as he did.

Frankie pulled her eyes away from his pecs. "I didn't say that," she denied hotly.

He gave her a smug, knowing smile. "You do not have to. I can see how you look at me."

Frankie's temper began to rise. "You are unbelievable."

"Thank you. I hear that a lot."

Her mouth dropped open at his arrogance and she shook her head. "I didn't mean it in a good way. Look, good talk, let's not rush to do this again." She spun on her heels and walked back up the aisle.

"I did not think you were the type to run away Frankie," he called after her, laughter in his voice.

"I'm not. I need to check on my friends." Her strides were not slowing down.

"Frankie?" His voice floated from behind her.

"What?"

"If I want something, I work hard till I get it," he warned her.

Frankie stopped, her hands balled by her side. How much more arrogant could he get? "Yeah, most guys do. It's just that they lose interest once they get it. Goodnight, Luciano." She didn't look back as she walked up the bunkhouse stairs.

CHAPTER 8

*I*t seemed surreal that they were loading the truck and horse trailer ready to haul Delila to the Need for Speed. They had decided to travel the day before to make sure the big buckskin mare had an opportunity to settle in and give good runs.

"Hey Frankie, is your gear bag the only thing left that you want packed?" called Deb.

"Yeah, mate." Frankie gave Delila one final stroke with the brush. "You're an old hand at how they run things here," she whispered as she picked up a rug. She placed it over Delila. "Do you think you can look after this little Aussie chick?"

Delila snorted as if in agreement. Frankie untied her lead rope and led her from her stall toward the trailer. The mare arched her neck in excitement as she stepped into the bright morning light.

"Are you guys ready for us?" Butterflies began to flutter in Frankie's belly, dancing wildly at the realization that hit hard. This was finally happening. They were headed to the Need for Speed World Championship.

"Sure am," called Gabi from the back of the truck. "Go ahead and load Delila up, and then we can get this show on the road." Delila loaded like the old hand she was, and Megan helped Frankie lift the ramp.

"How are you feeling?" Megan asked as she fastened the latch.

"Nervous, excited, kinda numb at the same time, as weird as that sounds."

"Sounds about right." Megan laughed. "I think I would be pooping my pants if I was in your boots."

"I packed spare jeans just to be safe." Frankie joined in her laughter. "Hey, I just need to do something. Can you tell the others I'll be a few minutes and then we can go?"

"Sure thing."

Frankie walked down the laneway that led to the last paddock yard. The big colt ambled over, ears pricked, eyes excited by the commotion up at the barn.

"Hey, big fella. I'm not going to be here for a few days, so I brought double the ration for you."

She held out two apples. He sniffed both as if pondering which one was the best before picking the chosen one up delicately. The fragrance of fresh apple mingled pleasantly with the odor of the horse as he chewed slowly. Frankie reached out and gave him a rub on his head, before offering up the second apple.

"Wish me luck," she said, leaving him to his snack.

The drive to the venue seemed both endless and surprisingly swift. Frankie hugged herself tightly in the passenger side of Gabi's truck, lost in the nervous, sick feeling that swamped her body. Around her, the girls' excited chatter swirled, amplifying her sense of disconnection. The confines of the truck began to feel suffocating, and Frankie longed to escape it. After what felt like an eternity, Gabi found a park and pulled in. Without a word, Frankie opened her door and got out, walking around to the trailer and entering to check on Delila. The mare's nostrils flared as the strange smells assailed her senses.

"Easy girl," crooned Frankie, hoping she sounded more confident than she felt.

"You ready for us to drop the ramp?" called Deb.

Frankie took a deep, steadying breath, her chest rising and falling. "Yep, good to go."

Delila emerged from the trailer as regal as any Queen. She swung her head around to assess the controlled chaos of the crowded parking lot before giving a loud snort. It was as if to say, *this is this best you've got*? Frankie admired the mare's ready acceptance of the situation and heartily wished she could somehow channel it.

"Delila has been allocated stall E21. Do you want to head over there, and we'll bring the rest of her gear?" Gabi asked.

"Sure." Frankie reached into the trailer to grab her mare's water bucket. "Meet you guys over there." She set off, trying act like she belonged. She had not gone more than a yard or two before Megan's voice whispered on the wind to her.

"I don't think I have ever seen her like this."

"It's a step up for Frankie. She was a big fish in a little pond back home. Here, she is a minnow in the Atlantic." Deb's voice now. "I love that girl, but now she needs to figure out if she has what it takes to be a winner or not."

As Frankie and Delila were swallowed up by the large building, a final voice reached her ears—Gabi's.

"There's a lot riding on it."

Frankie swallowed nervously at the Brazilian woman's words. The final part sent her anxiety rocketing.

"For everyone."

"Really?" Frankie groaned in frustration as the water

splashed from the bucket she had just set down in the stall, soaking the leg of her jeans.

Honestly, she didn't know whether to laugh or cry. Maybe in the interest of expediency, she could do both at the same time? Thank gosh Delila had settled in happily, already munching on the hay net Gabi brought over. The same Gabi now popped her head over the stall and laughed at her drenched state.

"You know they have showers here, right? No need to wash in a bucket of cold water."

"Very funny. I think you and Deb have been hanging out too much," Frankie replied sourly before grinning at her. "Some people are graceful under pressure. I just turn into a klutz."

"I've noticed. Especially around a certain handsome bull rider," teased Gabi.

"I have no idea who you are talking about."

"Tall dark and handsome, nice arse, and a smile that promises he knows what he's talking about."

"Still not ringing any bells." Frankie shook her head in mock confusion.

"Oh, Frankie, after all the girls that usually throw themselves at him, Luciano must wonder what to do with you." Gabi's eyes sparkled mischievously. "Or maybe that's the problem? You're wondering what he would like to do with you."

"Gabi!" Frankie threw the lead rope she had been holding at the laughing Brazilian girl, chuckling as she ducked out of harm's way. She gave Delila one final pat, promising her she would be back to check on her, and went in pursuit of her still chortling friend.

Frankie stared at the droplets of condensation that slid

down the side of her beer, colliding with each other in a race to the bottom. The night air had a distinct nip to it, a promise that fall would soon knock on summer's door. Earlier, their neighbors had wandered over and introduced themselves. On one side were an Argentinian qualifier and to the other, an American finalist. Both had seemed friendly in an assessing kind of way, making Frankie even more nervous as she realized how competitive everyone was.

The shrill ring of a phone jerked Frankie from her self-absorbed doldrums, her startled reflex causing her to splash her drink. Glancing around, she discovered it was Gabi's and settled back into her camp chair.

"Hey? Yeah, sure." Gabi held it out to Frankie. "It's for you."

"Huh?" Surprised, Frankie wiped her hand clean from any leftover beer residue and reached for the phone. "Hello?" Her stomach flipped as he spoke.

"Hola, Frankie." Luciano's voice was deep. "I wished to call to give you luck."

"Thank you," she blurted awkwardly, curious at the noise she could hear in the background. "Whereabouts are you?"

"I am in Columbus, Ohio, tonight. And tomorrow, I will be in Greensboro, North Carolina."

"Geeze, that's pretty full-on. I don't know how you can do that," she said in awe.

"It is what we do if we want to be champions," came his sage response.

Frankie found herself responding to this intriguing, deeper side of Luciano. Not to mention that it was a little hot —a big, tough bull rider that is in touch with his emotions. It wasn't something that Frankie was used to coming across. His words resonated with her.

"Are you feeling confident?" he asked.

"Let's see. So far, I have splashed water all over myself,

misjudged sitting down in a chair, and nearly walked into a barricade."

Luciano's deep baritone laugh sent a pleasant warmth spiraling into her stomach. "Oh, Frankie, your nerves are bad?"

"You could say that." She glanced up at her friends who suddenly seemed engrossed in the night sky. She stood up and walked a small distance away from her eavesdropping companions. "Sorry, I just had to move away. The girls are just about to fall off their chairs trying to listen."

"They care about you. So, these nerves, do you feel it in your belly?"

"Like I could spew more epically than in the *Poltergeist* movie," she emphatically declared.

"I do not get that reference, but I take it as yes?" he asked.

"That's a yes." In the background, she could hear voices and the crackle of the announcer. "I should let you go."

"In a minute. I wish to speak to you. Take a deep breath and think about how you will ride. See it in your mind. Really ride it. It is important to breathe. Are you doing this?"

Frankie closed her eyes and drew in a deep breath. "Breathing, check."

"Frankie, remember a champion thinks they are champ before they win the title. They believe."

"Is that why bull riders are all so arrogant?" she teased.

"If we did not think we could do it, it would be crazy to get on an angry bull, would it not?"

"Mate, it's bloody crazy no matter which way you look at it."

Once again, his abundant laughter warmed her through the phone. She heard muffled voices again, this time closer. "I will be there in a minute. Frankie, I have to go. Just remember, how to do what you Aussies say—she'll be right, mate."

"Luciano, ride like a champion tonight and be safe, okay?" She felt oddly in tune with him.

"I always do. But for you, tonight, I will be extra. Good-night, Frankie."

"Goodnight, Luciano." The phone line went dead, and Frankie was left with a remarkable sense of calm as she stared down at the phone. Maybe there was more to Luciano than just a sexy smile and a hot arse.

CHAPTER 9

*A*fter an unexpectedly good sleep considering all four girls slept sardined together in the trailer, Frankie awoke fresh and focused for what lay ahead. No one was more surprised than her at this since two of them snored so badly Frankie was surprised they didn't receive any noise complaints.

She had drawn number 216 in the run order for her first go round. The benefit was she didn't have too early a run. The bad thing was also that she didn't have too early a run. She spent the morning feeding up Delila and cleaning her stall before heading to the canteen to grab some breakfast. Afterwards, she took her mare for a walk around the grounds to give her a chance to stretch her legs.

Frankie watched as earlier competitors warmed up prior to entering the arena and witnessed their jubilation or dejection depending on how they went around the barrels. The steady pressure of nerves began to build up.

She closed her eyes and breathed deeply. In her mind's eye, she pictured Delila, her muscles rippling under her gleaming wheat-yellow coat, dancing in readiness to enter the ring. Her steadying herself in the saddle before urging the mare forward in the chute and Delila leaping willingly forward.

"Hey, too early for a snooze." Deb's voice broke through her vision.

"I was just trying something a friend told me about." The image vanished, lost to the fog of the far reaches of Frankie's mind.

"How are you feeling, mate?" Deb looked at her nervously.

"Actually, I'm good. In fact, I'm more than good. I'm ready to go kick some butt." Frankie was surprised to find it was true. The nerves she'd been battling had vanished as surely as her earlier daydream.

Relief washed over Deb's face. "That's good to hear. We were starting to worry that the pressure was getting to you."

Frankie smiled, her eyes glowing with excitement. "It was. Now I just want to go in there and show these Yanks exactly what an Aussie can do."

"I hope you don't mind, but I got this shirt made for you." Gabi held out an arena shirt. Brazilian green faded midway down into a navy blue. At the top of the design, the five stars of the Southern Cross sat beneath and slightly to one side of a blue globe sprinkled with twenty-seven white stars. "I wanted to show that we are in this together with you."

"Thank you, I love it." Frankie was genuinely moved. Gabi and her family had not only given her the opportunity to ride their precious mare, but had welcomed her and supported her in the weeks leading up to the event. "I came here to ride. I never knew I would make such a good friend as well." Her voice caught. "Ah, come here." She pulled Gabi into a quick hug.

"You'll make me cry! Now, go get changed, and let's do this."

Frankie quickly changed into the shirt. "How do I look?"

Gabi stepped forward and adjusted the collar. "Like a champion. Deb and Megan are already waiting inside. Delila is tacked up and ready. I think that is everything?" Her hands fluttered anxiously.

Frankie smiled at the other girl. "I thought I was the one that was meant to be nervous."

"Oh." Gabi's eyes lit up in remembrance. "I have a message for you." She handed Frankie her phone.

Last night, I kept up my end of the bargain and won. Breathe and ride like the champ you are. Good Luck. X

She smiled. So many people had faith in her, and it was time to start having a little herself. She walked to Delila and checked the cinch. "I'll see you on the flipside," she said, mounting smoothly.

The mare felt electric underneath her as she made her way to warm up. Although she loved Mac, Delila was next level in her ability and experience. She had been to big arenas and competed and it showed in her ready acceptance of the atmosphere that hummed around them. Before long, the steward called the next five girls to enter the chute, herself included.

One after the other, the girls in front of her went. Sometimes, the crowd roared their approval. Other times, they commiserated with the heartbroken cowgirl.

Before long, Frankie was at the head of the chute, the noise and everything around her fading into the background. She could feel the tension rise in Delila as she waited for her cue to run, her steps quickening in excitement.

With one final breath, she leaned forward. "We got this, girl."

The mare eagerly sprung away, the rails lining the chute blurring as she charged onto the arena. Somehow, they were no longer two separate beings, but became one harmonious unit until Frankie could no longer tell where she ended and the mare began. She felt Delila straining, looking for the first drum as she lined it up, neat around the first as she sent a shower of sand spraying, her muscles bunching beneath her rippling hide.

The second was taken care of in the exact same businesslike manner, Frankie sitting perfectly balanced, anticipating every movement. The last barrel neared, and she felt Delila lower herself boldly into the turn, her strong hindquarters digging in, tendons straining as they sought traction. Straightening, she flew toward the finish line, every ounce of horse and rider taut as they chased it down.

And then, as quickly as it began, it was done. The hollering and whooping of the crowd cascaded back into Frankie's awareness.

"Ladies and gentlemen, I would be very surprised if we don't see the Aussie Cowgirl back in the short go round later this evening." The announcer's strident voice crackled over the loudspeaker as Delila pounded down the chute, her momentum gradually slowing till she broke into a walk.

"Good girl. You're bloody marvelous. Good girl," praised Frankie, throwing both arms around her neck.

"Frankie!" Her friends waved excitedly as they jumped up and down. She happily waved back.

"That was an amazing round." Gabi hugged Delila as Frankie dismounted and loosened the cinch. "No matter what, you are guaranteed to be a finalist at Need for Speed."

"That's an awesome feeling. But you know what would be better? Wearing the championship buckle for Need for Speed," she shouted.

Deb raised her eyebrows as she looked to Megan and Gabi. "We might have created a monster here." She clapped Frankie on the shoulder. "But hey, personally, I'm all for an Aussie for the Champ."

～

Frankie ran her hand over Delila's legs, seeking signs of any heat or swelling. "Megan, I'm just going to trot her out. Can you have a quick check for any soreness?" The mare moved freely beside her as she jogged.

"Fit as a fiddle from where I'm standing," Megan said confidently.

"Excellent. Can't be too careful." Frankie let the mare pick at some grass. In an hour's time, the short go round would begin, drawn in order of time. Those with the slowest times ran first and the fastest times were last. Frankie was the third last to go, which meant she had an extra hour before the mare needed to get ready.

Gabi strode over, talking on the phone as she walked. "Yes, I'll get her. But I swear to the Almighty you need to get her number. Fine send her a Facebook request or something. Here, Frankie, it's lover boy." She thrust the phone into Frankie's hand.

Frankie went a brilliant shade of scarlet. "Um, hi."

"I have just gotten into Greensboro. Gabi tells me you are in the finals?" Luciano's rich voice filled her ear.

"Yep. Luciano, I think I can actually do this." She surprised herself with the confidence that rang out in her voice.

"You are there. First you think you're champion, then you become champ."

"In Australia, we call that faking it till you make it."

Luciano laughed. "I like that. I need to collect my gear bag. I just wanted to wish you luck. But maybe you don't need luck."

"Thanks. Good luck too, Luc." She hung up the phone and looked at three pairs of mirth-filled eyes staring at her. "What?"

"Good luck, Luc, we love you, Luc, mah, mah, mah!" All

three replied at the same time in sing-song voices, making gooey eyes and kissy faces.

"Are you done?" she said drily.

"Nope, not even a little." Deb turned to her comrades in mischief making. "What about you guys?"

Gabi gave Frankie a teasingly speculative look before taking pity on her. "Maybe we should wait till after tonight. But I may never be able to look Luc in the face again," she spluttered as the laughter exploded from her.

Delila's run in the final go round was as close to a carbon copy as you could get, with one important point of difference. Somehow, the wily mare managed an even faster time. Frankie's heart skipped a beat as she locked eyes on the clock to see her time was almost a second faster than the previous competitors. She handed Delila over to Gabi to cool down, quickly heading back to the holding pen to watch the last two girls run.

The girl from Argentina had made it into the finals and looked to be putting in a fast time till she knocked the last drum, putting Frankie into guaranteed second place and securing the buckle for best placed overseas rider on a loan horse. The final girl to run was American, and she would be tough competition riding her own horse and on home soil. All Frankie could do was pray the time she had posted would be fast enough and the other girl couldn't get near it.

The American flew into the arena, intent on the first can, around it clean. Her horse ate up the distance to the second around and left it standing. As they came into the last, her horse appeared to bog down in the sand, stalling for a moment before collecting himself again and heading for home.

But that was all it took for Frankie's time to stand.

"Ladies and gentlemen, this year's Need for Speed buckle winner is Frankie Smith from Australia. She also takes home the championship buckle for best placed overseas rider on a loan horse. Ladies and gentlemen, put your hands together and make some noise for the champ."

The rest of the evening flew by as if it was a surreal dream. By the completion of the awards ceremony, Frankie still had not fully processed that she had actually done it. Even with the very tangible evidence of her two trophy buckles as well as a trophy saddle, she could not comprehend that, after all of her hard work, she had done it. It was as if she was simply a spectator in her own body, locked in a stunned robotic stupor as she smiled and posed for photographs.

Gabi, Megan and Deb worked their way through the packed room toward her as she was being congratulated by a handsome, well-dressed gentleman in cowboy boots and a Stetson.

"I was just saying to Frankie that we would be interested in having some meetings with her once she decided what her next move is. Given how she rode here, we feel like her getting her Pro Card would be the next step for her."

Before Frankie could reply, Gabi stepped forward and offered her hand. "I'm Gabriella Cabrera, the owner of Affinity Ranch Stud and Frankie's business partner. The short-term plan is for Frankie to wrap up a few things back in Australia before she relocates permanently to the States to help train and compete our horses."

Frankie's eyes widened in surprise at Gabi's presumptuous statement. But if she was being totally honest, she found herself disinclined to correct the statement.

"Well, Gabriella and Frankie, this is my card. Once you are back and have set yourself up, give my secretary a call to arrange a meeting. I think we will be able to work well together." Giving each of the girls a firm handshake, he took his leave.

"What the heck just happened?" Deb looked between Gabi and Frankie in confusion.

"I'm kinda wondering that myself." Frankie arched a questioning eyebrow at Gabi.

Gabi had the grace to look embarrassed—if only slightly. A ruddy flush crept along her tanned cheeks before she raised her chin defiantly. "You weren't just going to go back home, back to whatever you all were doing, after all this," she cried, waving her hands to take in everything around them. "I can't believe that I'm the only one that thinks we could do something amazing together. With the horseflesh I'm breeding and you training and competing them, we could have a world class breeding and training ranch." Passion radiated from her.

Her passion resonated with Frankie as realization dawned on her. "You're offering me a job?" she asked incredulously.

"No. I'm offering you an equal partnership. Actually, I'm offering all of you an equal partnership," she corrected, drawing surprised gasps from Megan and Deb. "You're one of the best—if not *the* best—horsewoman I have ever seen. Even without being on the rodeo circuit, people would want horses trained by you. In all honesty, at some stage, with the right support and horseflesh, you will wear a gold NFR buckle. I can run the business side and match the bloodlines, and I was hoping to be on the road with you some of the time. That leaves the day-to-day running of the stud ranch, keeping horses in work and some of the time traveling with Frankie when I can't be there. I know she trusts you guys, so I was hoping you would fill those roles." She looked at each of the girls hopefully.

"Bloody heck," said Deb in amazement. "I don't know what to say."

"Well that's worth something. She normally doesn't shut up." Frankie grinned at her friend. "What do you think, Megan?"

"There are some cute guys over here." Megan winked at Deb.

"The food's good, but they don't have lamingtons or vegemite," replied Deb.

"They drive on the wrong side of the road, which Frankie can't seem to remember," countered Megan.

"That's true." Deb looked over at Gabi. "Would we get danger money for getting in the car with Frankie?"

Gabi looked at the Australian girls. "So, does that mean what I think it does?"

Frankie put her arms around her grinning friends, her own face split by a beaming smile. "Like a bindii in your sock." Laughing at Gabi's blank look, she tried again. "Looks like you're stuck with us."

CHAPTER 10

*T*he friends had returned to Australia and thrown themselves into what could only be described as controlled pandemonium. Both Deb and Megan had handed in their notice at their respective horse studs and would soon have the free time to finish packing. For Frankie, she had spent her day meeting with clients to give training notes and programs so they could transition over to new trainers. It was a draining process, as each visit ended in tears, hugs, and promises to come and visit.

Now she had only one visit left before she could head home and have a much longed-for beer to help her de-stress from her emotional day. Earlier, she had heard a promising young, up-and-coming cowgirl had lost her beloved horse, Snow. Frankie had known her family since she started in the Little Drummers class at local rodeos and had mentored her since.

"Frankie!" The teenage girl ran up, her arms open wide. Frankie wrapped her arms around her and lifted her off the ground.

"I won't be able to do that much longer, Chloe. You're

growing like a weed. Aren't you meant to stop once you're eighteen?" she said, laughing as she jostled her.

"Might have to put a brick on her head to stop her getting any taller." The older woman who had followed her out laughed. "I was so happy to hear that you won, Frankie. It's all Chloe talked about till—" She stopped, swallowing hard as she looked sadly at her daughter.

"Snow died." Chloe tried to appear grown up in her quiet acceptance of her horse's death. "Snakebite." Her voice trembled.

"Oh, honey." Frankie wrapped her arm around Chloe's shoulders. "I'm so sorry."

"It was horrible, Frankie. I found him, and there was blood coming from his nose. I didn't know what to do. But it didn't matter. He was already dead." The teenage girl sobbed.

"It's never easy to lose our horses. They're our best friends and know all of our secrets. So much more dependable than boys," Frankie consoled. "I have a favor I need to ask, Chloe."

"Anything, Frankie." Chloe sniffled.

Frankie laughed. "Maybe you should ask what it is first. I might need a hand with cleaning all the stalls before I go."

Chloe's mother joined the laughter, looking fondly at her daughter. "She would do it if you asked, Frankie. Now, if I asked, it would be a different story."

"Mum!"

"Well, good thing that's not the favor. I can't take Mac with me. He just isn't fast enough to run the times over there, and I won't be able to give him the attention he loves. It just wouldn't be fair. You know how much he loves to compete."

"He sure does. I love watching him run the barrels." Chloe's eyes glowed at the mental image of Mac flying around the arena.

"I don't want him sitting in a paddock waiting for me, either, 'cause I don't know when I'll be back. He's my best friend, and now it's time for him to be someone else's best friend. Maybe someone that needs one about now." Frankie looked intently at Chloe.

"Whoever gets him is going to be one lucky cowgirl, Frankie."

"You goose. She's talking about you, Chloe," said her mother.

"Me? Really, Frankie? You trust me with Mac?" And then Chloe cried, her slim shoulders shaking as she buried her face in her mother's shoulder. Losing her horse and gratitude for the unexpected gift crashed in on her.

From over her sobbing daughter's head, her mother mouthed a thank you.

"I need to get going, but I can drop him over tomorrow and show you how Mac likes everything run. You will need to know that if you will be his new servant. Oops, I mean owner," she said.

It was only as Frankie was driving home that she, too, began to cry. The tears flowed as the realization hit her. It was real. Tomorrow she would say goodbye to her horse, the only consolation being knowing how much Chloe would love him. She had never anticipated the high cost of chasing her dream.

The beer slid down her throat, icy cold as it took away the dryness her crying had left. Megan and Deb still weren't home, and Frankie spent time with Mac as he ate his feed. She tried not to fixate on it being the last time she would be privileged to do so. Bittersweet memories flooded her, making her throat thick with emotion. The awkward young gelding who had trouble moving all his hooves in the same direction and resembled a moose more than a horse as a two-year-old. When she had first started training him to race, getting around the drum had felt more like steering a cruise ship. The one positive had been that he took them so broad, there was no chance he would hit them!

"I thought I might find you here." Mitch's quiet voice broke through her thoughts.

"Yeah. Farewells, and all that. So, what are you doing here?" she asked stiffly.

"I probably deserve that. Frankie, I know you think I'm the world's biggest jerk, but I just wanted to come and say goodbye." Mitch thrust his hands into his jean pockets. "Look, Frankie, maybe I was a jerk for how I handled it, but I still think it was the right thing to do." He raised his chin defiantly.

"Right, for who?" demanded Frankie harshly, her brow wrinkled in protest. "So, you decide that it is best and then you ghost me? You didn't even have the balls to tell me why. I felt like such an idiot. You were the first guy that I liked, and you left me feeling like I did something wrong."

Mitch's lips flattened into a thin line as he absorbed her words. He took a step forward as if to take Frankie's hand in his before deciding better and raking his hand through his hair in frustration.

"I know I messed up. And honestly, I don't blame you for being angry. I wish I could go back and handle it better, but I can't. I was scared because I really liked you and knew that you were so out of my league. Maybe I ran away before you could," he finished softly, realization dawning on him.

Mac butted Frankie's hand in protest of her having stopped scratching him. She resumed her administrations, pondering Mitch's admission. Surprise filled her as she realized she no longer felt angry or hurt, just a lingering sadness.

She took another steadying sip of beer. "It's funny, Mitch. I've only been away for just under two months, and I feel nothing like that nervous girl. Gosh, I was such a klutz around you."

"I thought it was cute." He smiled hopefully.

"You were a jerk. And for the record, maybe not the world's biggest jerk, but definitely Australia's." She gave a sad little smile before she continued, this time much gentler. "But you were probably right. One day, when this ride I'm on settles down, I want kids. But weren't you still getting ahead of yourself after just one kiss?"

Mitch stared at her intently. "You really didn't know, did you?" he asked softly. "Just how much I liked you?"

A slow ache filled her chest as thoughts flashed through her mind of what could have been. "I think I was too inexperienced to think the guy I had a crush on could want something serious with me."

He took her chin gently in his hand, tipping her head up to look him in the eye. "One day, Frankie I hope you realize just how special you are." He kissed her gently on the forehead. "Do you think we can be friends again?"

"I think we are already on our way."

"Good," he said, his expression breaking into a relieved smile. "Maybe I should leave before I can stuff it up."

"That's a good idea. Why don't you do that?"

Mitch gave her a mock salute. "Yes, captain." He turned to leave.

"Oh, and Mitch? Maybe next time, don't presume a girl just wants you for your kid-making abilities," she suggested. "Who knows, maybe you have more to offer." She shrugged with a sly smile.

In every fork-in-the-road moment in life, there is a point where you are in the dead center of that decision. You could turn back, and maybe that would be safer, or you can take a deep breath, hold your nose, and jump. Luckily, Frankie wasn't jumping alone.

The barn was eerily quiet, all traces of sawdust removed in readiness for the new tenants to move in. No familiar bay head begging for treats or restless movements of new horses settling in. It was unnerving how quickly any evidence of them having ever been here had been erased. It seemed unfair, as if such a critical time should somehow have imprinted itself into the very fabric of the building.

"It's hot out there." Deb stepped in from the bright sunlight. "I'm glad. I'd like to remember this place with the sun shining on my back and the sky clear and blue."

"It's azure."

"Frankie, we've had this discussion before. Blue is blue." Deb looked at her friend curiously. "How are you feeling?"

"Like I want to stay here, not moving, forever. I'm scared and sad. Don't get me wrong, I'm excited too, and I know this is a great opportunity. But what if I'm not good enough? What if winning that one race was all the grace I will get, and now I am reaching further than I was meant to? And to try for more is to just fall crashing down? I feel like I can't breathe past all the doubt," Frankie blurted out in a rush.

"Frankie, there are a lot of people who believe in you. But that means nothing if you don't bloody believe in yourself." The honk of a car horn sounded outside. Deb gave her hand a sympathetic squeeze. "That's the taxi. I'll get our bags loaded."

Frankie took one last breath as if the lingering fragrances of days past could banish the doubts from her head. She brushed her hand gently along the top of Mac's stall door and found some stray tail hairs he must have rubbed out curing himself of an itch. She gently tugged them free, deciding as she looked down that she hadn't come this far and said goodbye to so much to run scared now. Placing the hairs in her pocket, she farewelled her past and turned, determinedly walking toward her future.

CHAPTER 11

*T*he day had been arduous and emotionally draining. Frankie wasn't even sure if such an extended period spent traveling could even be called a day. It sure as heck felt longer. The Cabreras had been welcoming on their arrival with a small feast prepared as the guests of honor were welcomed back into the bosom of the family.

Her friends had crashed long ago, their jet lag finally catching up with them. But Frankie couldn't slip into sleep's welcoming embrace. She found her feet leading her down past the row of stalls, past the dozing Delila, until she stopped in front of the colt. He cocked an ear at her arrival but otherwise ignored her presence, preferring instead to return to his slumber.

Frankie's phone buzzed, causing the colt to open his eyes and glare at the interruption. She looked down to find Luciano's name displayed on the screen.

"Hello." She was surprised at how drained her voice sounded.

"Ola, Frankie. I am sorry it is late, but I have just finished my rides. Welcome back." Luciano's voice was hard to hear over the cheering crowd in the background.

"It's, um, good to be back." She strained to hear. "How did you do tonight?"

"I rode only the one for time." She could practically hear his shrug through the phone. "Still enough to be in the checks."

Frankie tried in vain to stifle a yawn and failed spectacularly. "I'm sorry for yawning in your ear like that. That's awesome work tonight." Another yawn overcame her.

"Frankie, Querida, go to sleep."

She chuckled in agreement, perplexed by what querida meant. "I think I might have to. Thanks for thinking of me."

"Querida—" *There it was again!* "I have been thinking about you since I first met you. Maybe tonight you will dream about me?"

"Honestly, tonight I'm too tired to even dream about sleeping." She yawned again for dramatic effect. "Good night, Luc."

"Goodnight, Frankie." His voice wrapped around her as intimately as if he held her. "I will be home soon."

Frankie shivered in anticipation of his words as she hung up the phone.

The following morning after a hearty breakfast at the main house, the girls settled down to hash out their business plan and designate roles and duties. It was quickly agreed that Frankie's primary focus was to be competing and training the young stock as they came through. She would serve as the brand's public face, an example of just what the Affinity Ranch Stud horses could achieve. Gabi was to continue selecting and matching bloodlines and looking after the business side, as well as travel with Frankie as her manager. Deb and Megan were jointly allocated the role of stud managers and keeping horses in work.

Gabi clapped her hands in satisfaction. "Now that's all decided, let's get to work."

As Frankie readied Delila in the barn, Gabi bustled over, her phone in hand. "Frankie, when you've finished with Delila, we need to sit down and work out a travel schedule for you. I've also made contact with Bryce Dougson, you remember him? He talked to you about sponsorship."

"I remember him, he seemed nice." Frankie knelt to put her horse's boots on.

"He's nice, but he's also the CEO of the largest western wear company in the States. They want us to come in next week with our travel plans for the next twelve months to go over with them." Gabi scrolled through her emails as she spoke.

Frankie rubbed the back of her neck before standing, feeling slightly too hot as the reality hit her. It was all or nothing now. "You are the next thing on my to-do list, then. Are you coming to watch?"

"I can't this morning. There's so much to do. It's exciting to actually start getting our name out on the circuit." Gabi bounced a little on her feet in anticipation.

Frankie fiddled with the straps on her mare's bridle. "Gabi, what does querida mean?"

The Brazilian looked at her, a teasing twinkle in her eyes. "Let me guess where, or should I say whom, you heard that from. Cute bull rider?"

"Yeah. Now can you please tell me what it means?" Frankie pleaded, embarrassed.

"It means sweetheart. Luciano called you his sweetheart," Gabi said, the last in a sing-song voice.

Frankie bit her lower lip. "I'm not sure what to do with that information."

"Well, I don't think Luciano has a habit of going around calling every girl he meets querida if that says anything." Gabi raised her eyebrows speculatively as she looked at her.

"Frankie, he likes you. Now what are you going to do about that?"

Frankie untied Delila. "I'm going to go train my horse."

"Coward," Gabi called after her.

"Really?" Frankie muttered under her breath, watching the big Ford Black Ops truck pull up.

After her conversation with Gabi, it was hard not to feel under siege to now have Luciano appear in the flesh. Both he and Joao climbed out of the truck as Senhor Eduardo came to greet them, clasping the men's hands firmly. Luciano flashed a smile her way as if instinctively knowing she was staring. Pulling her eyes away, she decided the best course of action was to ignore their arrival. She returned her attention to Delila and the exercise she had set up.

But she did take pause when she saw Senhor Eduardo go down to catch the colt from his paddock and bring him up to where the men stood. The colt excitedly pranced on the lead, giving little half rears and snorts at the unexpected freedom from his yard. Gabi walked over to the arena, watching the commotion as well.

"What's going on, Gabi?" She raised her eyebrows as she nodded in the colt's direction.

"Papai has been talking about selling the colt, maybe he is showing him to Joao and Luciano. He always says he can't be trusted. Maybe he thinks one of those cowboys can manage him. It's a shame. If someone could get him to work with them, not fight against them, he could be a champion," Gabi said sadly.

A cold ball of dread settled in Frankie's stomach at the thought of not seeing the colt again. She walked Delila toward the gate, nodding her thanks as Gabi opened it for her.

It all happened so fast. From the corner of her eye, she saw the already fractious colt pull back abruptly, dragging the lead rope from Senhor Eduardo's hands. Before anyone could react, the colt spun and bucked, kicking a hind leg aimed at the men, before bolting down the drive. Without hesitation, Frankie urged her mare after the colt, flying past the men climbing into Luciano's truck.

The colt had made it onto the dirt road before he suddenly realized he was no longer in familiar territory. His mad bolt slowed, and he continued to snort and buck, his eyes wide. Frankie pulled Delila up and slid off her.

"Hey, big boy," she said soothingly, holding her hand out as she slowly walked toward him. The colt released a loud snort, his white flecked sides heaving. "Easy." Frankie took it as a good sign the colt had stopped his restless movement to watch her. From behind, she was dimly aware that Luciano had pulled his truck up at the end of the drive and was motioning for the other men to wait. The colt continued to observe her steady advance, his muscles trembling.

"I swear to you, big duffer, if you let me catch you, I'll give you all the apples I can get my hands on. You'll have apples for days," she crooned. He lowered his head to sniff her outstretched hand, nostrils flaring. "Almost there," she whispered as she reached her other hand slowly for the lead rope. The colt let out a long sigh as if to release all the pent-up nerves that had coursed through his body during his madcap escape as her hand closed around the lead. He dropped his head and let her pat his lathered neck. "Okay, mate, let's head for home."

As she led the colt and Delila past the men, she saw Luciano turn to Senhor Eduardo. "That girl has a gift, maybe she is the one who is meant to ride him. Maybe they are each other's destiny."

She was sure Senhor Eduardo gave Luciano an incredulous look. "I thought you liked the girl? Maybe I was wrong."

"It's because I like her you should listen. You have eyes. I don't think he will hurt her."

Frankie couldn't help but smile. A smile that slipped from her face at the words that followed.

"While I own him, I can't risk her getting hurt."

The rest of Senhor Eduardo's words were lost on the wind as she led the horses away, feeling Luciano's gaze following her.

Frankie shuddered against the sudden chill that beset her, frustrated that no one understood that all he needed was a chance, heck they both deserved the chance.

Frankie's friends waited in the barn, a gathering of nervous energy for her return. Gabi took Delila, and Megan helped unsaddle her. Frankie walked the colt to the wash bay and began to hose off his sweat-lathered coat. The veins still bulged beneath his hide.

"Hey, Deb, can you go and see if we have any apples and grab a few for me if we do?" she said, then whispered to the colt. "A deal is a deal." After scraping the excess water off, she led him to his stall. "I think you have had quite enough adventures for one day." She took his halter off and gave him a final pat, closing the stall door behind her.

Slowly, she fed him the apples Deb managed to rustle up. The colt, suddenly alert, stopped mid-chew. She turned to see Luciano striding down the aisleway.

"That was quite the display," he said by way of greeting.

"Nah. Everyone thinks he's as mad as a cut snake. But I think it's just an act." Frankie laughed at Luciano's baffled expression.

"I am not familiar with this saying."

"You know, not playing with a full deck? A few stubbies short of a six-pack? One sandwich short of a picnic?" she explained. "One wave short of a shipwreck? Loco?"

Enlightenment dawned over his features. "Yes, we think he is crazy."

"Well, he's not. If someone just gave me a chance, I could prove it." Passion rang clearly in her voice. "But no one will listen."

"I believe you could do it."

His words stopped Frankie mid-spiel. "What?"

"I have asked Senhor Eduardo if I may buy him. If he agrees, I will give you your chance. On one condition—if I think it is too dangerous, that is the end," he warned, looking at Frankie for her response.

"No worries, she'll be right."

Luciano leaned forward, his eyes serious. "I mean it, Querida."

"Fine," huffed Frankie, crossing her arms crankily.

He smiled smugly. "You are very cute mad. Now shall we go to the house and join the others?"

It was only then Frankie realized her friends had deserted her. *Geeze, thanks guys.* Exasperated, she let Luciano guide her from the barn.

As usual, Sra Cabrera's food was delectable, the rich aromas rising off the dishes causing Frankie's stomach to rumble. She wasn't aware Sra Cabrera was planning a cooked lunch. This was so much better than the sandwich she had been planning on having.

Luciano's hand, warm on her back, gently guided her in front of him to the table. Deb gave Frankie a teasing smile when she noticed Luciano's attentive demeanor. Frankie selected her food and quickly took a seat between Gabi and Megan, leaving Luciano to sit across the table. He raised questioning eyebrows at her sudden abandonment before grinning in acceptance.

"Frankie, we still need to talk about the schedule," Gabi said, interrupting the connection between the two of them.

"I'm free as soon as I finish eating," Frankie muttered around a mouthful of food.

"Maybe I need to make my appointment with you now before you are too busy," Luciano said.

Frankie gulped down her food, choking slightly. "Um, what appointment?"

"I would like you to come and see my ranch," he said.

"Is ranch a euphemism?" Deb whispered.

"I hope so," Megan murmured, clearly enjoying herself. "He can show me his ranch any time he wants." She pretended to fan herself.

"I'm sitting right here," Frankie muttered under her breath to her friends.

"I wonder if it is true, everything is bigger in Texas?" Deb curiously speculated.

"Guys!" pleaded Frankie.

"Leave her alone," said Gabi taking pity on Frankie. "She still needs to answer him, and yes *everything* is bigger in Texas."

Frankie looked sheepishly at Luciano, who had clearly heard every word of their whispered conversation and was doing his best not to laugh at her embarrassment. "When were you thinking of doing it?"

He looked at Gabi for permission. "Is she free tomorrow?"

She checked her phone. "I don't have anything booked in for her."

"Good. I will pick her up after lunch," he nodded his head decisively. "I look forward to showing you around, Querida."

"Eager little bugger, isn't he?" whispered Deb.

"Doesn't waste time," agreed Megan.

"Have you guys finished?" Beet red, Frankie attempted to return to her meal.

"I think so." Deb turned to Gabi. "Now, let's talk about you and Joao."

CHAPTER 12

*L*uciano's shiny black truck pulled up at precisely the exact moment Frankie finished eating her sandwich. She was beyond grateful that, for once, her friends were nowhere to be seen, she wasn't sure her nerves would have been able to take it.

Luciano stepped out looking like a cowgirl's pin-up in freshly starched jeans, a championship buckle, boots, and a fitted black V-neck T-shirt. He doffed his hat when he saw her standing at the stairs to the bunkhouse, the light glinting off his raven locks. Frankie's stomach flipped at the warmly possessive look he sent her way.

"Are you ready, Frankie?" he strode toward her, his megawatt smile on full display.

"Like a convict heading to the gallows." She smiled merrily at his confused look. Gosh dang, he looked hot with the way he cocked his head to one side as he considered whatever she said. "I'm ready," she clarified.

He guided her to his truck, opening the door for her and waiting until she was safely inside before closing it and moving to the driver's side. As the motor roared into action, Frankie's nerves slammed through her body, robbing her of all confidence. Suddenly, the warmth of his hand was on hers. She looked at him, startled.

"Relax, Querida, I will not let anything happen to you."

Frankie let out a shaky laugh. "That obvious, hey?"

"Querida, I like you and very much wish you to see my ranch. But if you do not want to do this, I can turn around. Maybe we do it another day?" His voice was gentle as he spoke.

Frankie closed her eyes, steadying her nerves. "I'm being silly. It's just, I don't really go on dates," she said by way of explanation. "And well, you are you." She lamely gestured at him with her hand.

He laughed. "Of course I am me. Who else would I be?"

"You're a whole lot of man to take in."

He gently stroked the back of her hand with his thumb in a circular motion. A tingling sensation sent a shiver through Frankie, chasing the nerves from her body and replacing it with another type of tension entirely.

"You are a beautiful, strong woman, and you deserve a man, not some little boy." He gave her a suggestive side glance. "I think you like how much man I am."

Frankie's cheeks flamed. "Maybe I just don't know what to do with it."

The look he cast her way was pure masculine ego. "I would be more than happy to show you."

She was saved from having to reply as they turned into a drive. The long gravel laneway opened to what she had quickly discovered was the traditional layout of the house, barn and machinery shed. As the truck pulled to a stop, Luciano smiled at her. "Welcome to minha casa, my home."

Frankie looked around curiously. Everything was meticulously maintained and cared for. Luciano obviously took pride in his ranch. "It looks lovely."

He walked around and opened the truck door. Frankie slid out, conscious of how close he was. The cowboy reached down and took her hand, enveloping it in his much larger one. "I had thought, first, we do a tour of the ranch land, and then I will show you the house and we can have dinner."

"Oh, that sounds like a good plan," Frankie rushed out, a little too quickly.

That mischievous smile appeared on Luciano's swarthy face. "Trust me, Frankie, where you are concerned, I have a lot of good plans," he promised, leading them to a parked quad bike. "I would like to know your thoughts on my ranch."

He proudly showed her through paddocks and laneways, grassy fields and treed woods until they emerged into a clearing, the sprawling vista before them. "This is the boundary of the ranch."

Frankie climbed off the back of the quad bike, reverently looking at the landscape laid out before her eyes. "It's beautiful, Luc."

His closeness made her tremble as he stepped closer and gently wrapped his arms around her. "You are beautiful," he murmured, his breath warm on her neck.

Frankie could feel the hardness of his body as he held her snug in the warm cocoon of his embrace. Her nerves, hypersensitized by the promise of his touch, sent ripples of yearning cascading from her stomach as she found herself anticipating his caress. He gently brought his hand to her cheek, delicately tracing the line of her jaw with a workroughened thumb that sent shivers skipping down Frankie's spine. Spellbound by his nearness, she was helpless to look away as he gently guided her face to his, the musky aroma of him intoxicating her senses as he tilted her chin up. He lowered his head and tenderly kissed her, the world fading away till there was nothing but Luciano. The passion that lay beneath was tantalizing, and his lips were surprisingly soft against hers. As he slowly withdrew from the kiss, his eyes searched her face, an unspoken question plain in his look.

Frankie smiled at him shyly, still ensconced in his warmth. "That was nice."

He returned her smile, smug male arrogance once again on full display. "Nice, Querida? Next time, I will melt your bones."

Dust mites danced playfully in the early morning rays of sunlight that flittered into Frankie's room. She stretched languidly, catlike in her movements. It took her a moment to pinpoint the precise source of her current mood. Luciano's kiss yesterday at the ranch! A delicious warmth filled her at the memory of his soft lips on hers, the possessive look in his eyes as he promised her more.

Deciding her present line of thought would only cause frustration, she threw the bedcovers back and rolled out of bed. Padding softly to the coffeepot, she poured herself a steaming cup of the pungent brew. She cradled the warm cup in her hands, blowing softly on it, her mind once again drifting back to Luc. The creak of Deb's bedroom door jolted Frankie back to the present, scattering her thoughts as if dandelions on the breeze. She poured another coffee and wordlessly handed it to her friend.

Deb peered at her with sleepy eyes as she took a bracing sip. "I take it from that dreamy little smile that everything went well yesterday?"

Frankie couldn't stop her joyous smile from appearing. "It was nice." Her expression was coy before she gave in. "He kissed me."

"I figured something happened from the way you are beaming all over the place, which it's way too early for," Deb grumbled. "So, how was it?"

"It was nice." She casually sipped her coffee.

"If Luciano hears all of this describing him as nice, I'm sure he'll be offended," Deb noted.

"I already told him his kiss was nice."

"What's nice?" Gabi asked, walking into the kitchen.

"Luciano's kisses are, apparently," Deb said, filling her in.

"He kissed you?" Gabi said excitedly.

"Who kissed who?" Yawning, Megan joined the friends and poured herself a mug.

"Is everyone here now?" Frankie threw her hands in the air in mock frustration.

Deb gave a quick look around. "I think so. Unless you want me to get Senhor Eduardo and Sra Cabrera." She looked at Gabi. "Do you think we should?"

"Oh my gosh," Frankie cried dramatically, putting her head on the kitchen table.

"Is she having some kind of fit?" asked a concerned Gabi, her eyes opened wide.

"Probably, but don't worry. She is prone to dramatic fits, if you hadn't noticed." Unconcerned, Deb poured herself another cup of coffee.

"Tell me again why I thought it was a good idea to go into business with you guys," Frankie said.

"Because you love us." Megan leaned forward. "Now, back to this kiss. We want all the juicy details."

CHAPTER 13

*T*he black colt, his sweat stained coat appearing iridescently oily, flicked his head agitatedly as he kicked out angrily toward the human. The slender girl stood in the precise center of the round pen, relentlessly driving him forward, watching, waiting, for any sign that the colt was abandoning his resistance to her.

Relaxing her body, she patiently stood, waiting for the horse to register that she was no longer driving him forward. Gradually, the mad run changed from gallop to lope, his ear twitching toward her, undecided whether to trust her or not.

"Easy boy," Frankie crooned.

The colt shuffled a few strides of a jog before he slowed to a walk, chewing as he sized her up. Seeing no threat, he left the edge of the pen, his nostrils flaring with each breath he took. Head lowered in acceptance, he finally submitted.

She wiped her sweaty brow before stroking his lathered hide. "You're a stubborn one, but boy are you strong. Strong in body and in spirit and if you're going to be the champion I think you are, well you're going to need it in spades. Maybe I should call you Sampson."

The newly minted Sampson let out a soft sigh of acceptance for his human, before nudging her for more pats. Frankie laughed as she led him toward the gate.

"Your uncle Mac used to say and do the same thing." She felt a twinge of homesickness thinking of her old companion. "Anyway, I think you'll find that you and I are going to get along just fine, and maybe set the world on fire while we're at it."

~

Frankie rested on the steps of the bunkhouse, her head reeling as she nursed a cold beer. She wryly noted that all the stress was driving her to drink. Her neck stiff and her muscles strained, she processed the meeting she had earlier attended with Gabi at the Black Angus Western Wear Headquarters. Bryce, the CEO they had met at the Need for Speed Championship had been as good as his word. His company was offering her an incentive sponsorship with the aim of her getting a Pro Card.

To be fair, Frankie had simply sat there, nodding at the appropriate times while Gabi took control, discussing proposed schedules. It wasn't that Frankie didn't care. She understood just how vital the sponsorship was for their fledgling stud, but it was more that Frankie was happiest when she was riding, not in a boardroom. On the other hand, Gabi was proving she thrived on it.

Frankie twisted the end of her ponytail around her finger, wondering what the next few months would bring.

"It cannot be so bad." Luc's warm voice, smooth as molasses, interrupted her thoughts.

She looked up to see the cowboy had materialized in front of her while she was engrossed in her stressing. She smiled at him and the familiar breathless feeling swept over her.

"I saw these while I was moving the steers and they made me think of you." He produced a bouquet of wildflowers from behind his back and offered them to her.

Frankie stood, her eyes sparkling as she accepted the bundle. The bouquet was a riot of blues, reds and oranges. She recognized bluebonnets, fireweeds, and Indian paintbrush.

"They are gorgeous," she breathed, staring down at them in her hands, not sure what to do next.

Luciano had no such concerns as he stepped forward, gathered her into his arms and kissed her. "I have been thinking about doing that all day."

Frankie was breathless as she sunk down, not only from his kiss, but his nearness. It was impossible to be around his magnetic presence and remain unaffected. "Pull up a pew," she said inanely.

"Now, are you going to tell me what the reason is for your frown?" he asked gently, sitting down on the step beside her.

"We met with some sponsors today. You know Black Angus?" She fiddled with the petal of a flower.

"Yes, they are my major sponsors. Bryce is a good man. He will look after you." Luc put his arm comfortably around her.

"I didn't know they sponsored you." Surprised, she took another sip of her beer.

Luc took the bottle from her and had a long drink. Frankie, her lips still moist, was mesmerized by the sight of his lips touching the cool glass, his eyes half-closed in enjoyment.

"Why are you worried about this meeting? Did it not go well?" His brow crinkled in concern. "I can give them a call and see what I can do?"

Frankie momentarily lost her train of thought as she

watched him lick a drop of beer from his lip. "Oh, it's not like that. It went well. They've offered me an incentive sponsorship, which Gabi is stoked about," she rushed to explain. "I guess that's maybe it. Gabi has put so much effort into getting this deal and sorting out schedules and everything. What happens if I let her down?"

He gave her shoulder a gentle squeeze and pulled her closer, her denim-clad thigh snug against his. "Gabi has her dreams to make this stud great. You have your dream to be champion. Together, I think you will both get what you want. Both of you have talents. All you need to do is keep doing what you are doing."

Frankie turned his words over in her mind, finding comfort in them. "That helped," she admitted.

He turned her face toward his, a sensuous turn to his mouth. "I know something else that will help." He leaned down, his face close to hers.

"Yeah?" Frankie said softly, her eyes twinkling with mischief. Her heart beat faster in anticipation. "Whatever could you have in mind Senhor Navarro?"

"It is better if I show you." He waggled a finger sternly at her. "And this time, I don't want to hear *nice*."

CHAPTER 14

*T*he cab of the truck held the stale, dank smell that only too many miles traveled in too short a time can do. Frankie shifted in her seat, trying to arrange her limbs to ease the dull cramp beginning to build in her calf. Outside, the endless expanse of tundra flashed past her windscreen, and the soft snoring of Gabi sleeping beside her in the passenger seat provided a rhythmic soundtrack.

It had been a tough few weeks as Frankie went through her baptism of fire, hauling Delila to rodeos and chasing a Pro Card. Although Frankie didn't care to admit it, especially to herself, Luciano had been the one to help her get through the physically and emotionally draining new experience.

No matter where they were, or which state Luc had been in, he had always found the time to call. It was his calm, wise words of experience from years of almost constant travel that had been key to Frankie keeping her sanity. When all else failed, his teasing was almost guaranteed to drive her doubts away with her laughter.

Now, as the miles disappeared, the bitumen eaten up by the relentless turn of the truck tyres, they would be home soon. And with it, two weeks of blessed rest from the road.

Luc had already told her he would be home for most of that time. Just the thought of being in the same state—of being able to touch him—sent a flutter of electricity through Frankie.

"Thinking about Luciano again?" mumbled a sleepy Gabi. "Or is there someone else that is putting a smile on your face?"

Frankie laughed. "What can I say? Maybe I missed that arrogant Brazilian cowboy." She shrugged. "But only a little."

"I can't believe that, if you and Delila keep going like you have the last couple of weeks, you guys will have filled your Pro Card. Then the real work starts."

Frankie forced herself to relax her suddenly tight grip on the steering wheel. "I wonder if the nerves ever get better."

"Probably not." Gabi gave her a sly, sideways wink. "Just to keep you on your toes. Speaking of which, it's been almost a week since you last tried to drive on the wrong side of the road."

"Shut up." Frankie slapped her friend on the leg. "You can't be too worried—the amount you sleep while I drive." She straightened in her seat. "Look, Gabi. We're here." She saw the ranch gate come into view.

It was good to be home.

Gabi got off the phone with Black Angus, her giddy excitement spilling over, contagious to the others even before she could share the source of her elation.

"Oh. My. Gosh!" she said dramatically, enunciating each word. "Looks like Frankie is going to be a supermodel." A flurry of excitement met her announcement.

"What? When?" Frankie asked through the racket, the nerves starting. Her fingers twisted in a knot.

"Black Angus wants to do an advertising campaign with

you and—drum roll please." Megan and Deb tapped the table enthusiastically. "Thank you, maestros." Gabi paused for dramatic effect. "Luciano."

Apparently satisfied with their reactions, she continued. "It seems word has gotten out that you will be campaigning a horse for him and they think it would be a good story for the public. Something like *Brazilian bull rider helps poor up-and-coming Australian Barrel Rider achieve her dreams*." Gabi paused thoughtfully, rubbing her chin in reflection. "I wonder if there's a movie in that, or the very least a romance novel?" She shook her head to clear her thoughts. "Now, where was I? That's right. Anyway, they want you there tomorrow."

Frankie collapsed into her chair. "Oh, no," she blurted out. Gabi looked at her in confusion. "But what will I wear?"

Frankie figured supermodel hours weren't all that different to cowgirl hours. The incessant beeping of her alarm had momentarily made a confusing appearance in her dream of Tim Tams and dishwashers before she groggily woke enough to turn it off. For a moment, she wondered if all models had such weird dreams before deciding that, at the very least, food must feature fairly consistently in their fantasies.

Hurrying to have a quick shower before Luc arrived to drive them to the shoot, Frankie silently thanked her friends for covering her share of the ranch work. And at the same time, cursing them when she heard their peaceful snoring. It might not have quite been an accident when she slammed the door a little too hard as she stepped into the still dark morning. Too early even for the faintest of colors to paint the sky.

A toasty warmness enveloped her as she stepped up into Luc's Black Ops Truck, the fragrant aroma of coffee wafting through the cab. She leaned across and gave her cowboy a quick morning kiss, before settling back into her seat. He handed her a travel mug.

"Here, Querida. I thought you might need this."

She gratefully accepted, the dark elixir evoking alertness in her otherwise befuddled state of mind. "Thanks, Luc. Are these things always so early?"

"Most of the time, yes. This is the first shoot I have done that has not been with another bull rider. Maybe they think a woman will take longer to get ready for cameras?" he joked.

Frankie almost sprayed coffee out her nose as she spluttered her indignation.

"Easy, Frankie. I'm not saying that is what I think. But you never can tell with photoshoot people." He displayed no genuine remorse for his teasing.

"Luc, you're not helping." Her nerves forced themselves to the forefront of her mind. "I think I want to be sick."

Luciano swiftly pulled the truck over. Not before he put her window down, she sourly noted. "Querida, you have nothing to worry about. You are a beautiful woman." He squeezed her hand reassuringly. "Plus, I will be there. Did you know, if I did not become a bull rider, I would be a professional model?"

Against Frankie's inclination, she began to laugh. "Okay, Fabio. Let's get going so you can show me how the camera loves you."

And boy did the camera love him, but not half as much as the hair and makeup people, or the stylist, or the photographer, for that matter. It had been a long day of posing and, unexpectedly for Frankie, waiting around. She sat glumly in the makeup chair as they changed her hair for the last look of the day. It would probably have gone faster if the hairstylist could stop drooling over Luciano with the makeup artist.

"Look at those thighs." Tash, the makeup artist, breathed in admiration.

"He can wrap those things around my—" Thankfully,

Doug's—the makeup artist—comment was cut off by the stylist's approach.

"Frankie, this one is a little different. The outfit we have chosen for this is a softer, more romantic look. We think we should be able to time it right and get the sunset in the background. Bob will tell you exactly what he wants once you're ready."

Frankie obediently went to change, careful not to smudge anything. Luciano's eyes widened as he caught sight of her hesitantly walking toward him. Delicious warmth filled her body at the possessive gleam that flickered in his eyes.

Bob, the photographer, gave her a nod of approval. "Now, in this one, I want to try for something different. We only have about two minutes, if that, to get these colors of the sunset. I want this to be more tender, more emotional," he instructed. "If you can both stand over there, we can start."

Frankie stood stiffly beside Luc as directed, pondering how best to interpret Bob's instructions. "I'm not sure exactly what you want." She battled a twinge of anxious confusion.

"Frankie, you are a woman, he is a man. You are here in a beautiful place, with a beautiful sunset. Just work with that a bit," Bob encouraged.

She felt Luc's hand fit snuggly into the small of her back, before he bowed his head closer to hers. "Good, Luciano. Frankie, I need you to be more natural," the photographer called. Luciano's hand slid lower down her back until it had a firm hold on her arse. She looked up at him, a sparkling challenge in her eyes.

"Excellent," Bob said around his laughter. "Not what I had in mind, but original."

Luciano pulled Frankie in closer, his eyes devouring her face. "Querida, ignore them. There is no one here but you and I." She could feel the warmth of his palms on her waist. "Relax and look at me."

She raised her eyes to meet his, overwhelmed at what she

saw. He lowered his head and kissed her tenderly as they stood silhouetted against the gloriously vibrant hues of red blended with oranges, purples, and crimsons.

Frankie was only distantly aware of the clicking of Bob's camera as he muttered his approval. When the kiss finally ended, it was with smug satisfaction that she saw the disgruntled looks leveled her way by Tash and Doug.

CHAPTER 15

*B*lack clouds sprawled across the sky, billowing in from the west. In the distance, a low crackle of thunder rolled, a streak of hot silver splitting the sky.

"Might get some rain," Luc observed as they headed for home.

In the passenger seat, Frankie was still reeling, intoxicated from Luciano's bold tenderness at the photoshoot.

"That didn't end up too bad," she mused, gently biting her full lower lip.

"The rain?" he glanced at her questioningly.

"The photoshoot. Everyone was so excited that I was doing it, but honestly, I was kinda dreading it." She hugged herself absently. "I'm glad I did it."

"It was a good idea of mine to do this campaign then?"

She looked at him flabbergasted, her brows shooting skyward. "What did you say?"

"It was time for me to do another campaign for Black Angus, and I suggested that I might like to do one with you. Bryce liked it." He glanced at Frankie. Finding no obvious signs of protest, he returned his focus to the road.

"Oh," Frankie said, a slight catch in her voice. "So, they didn't want me?" She was gutted by his revelation.

"Querida, you are their sponsored rider too. They wanted you. I just suggested a way to work together." Frankie mulled his answer over, looking for a reason to find insult, but could find none.

Outside, the tree branches swayed in the strengthening winds, surrendering their leaves without a fight. The truck rocked with each gust. On the far hill, a jagged bolt of white-hot lightning slashed the sky, the thunder seconds behind. Frankie jumped at the noise.

"Thank gosh we're nearly home," she shouted, trying to be heard over the noise.

Luciano captured her hand in his calm hold, his hand steady. "I will get us there safely, Frankie. I promise I won't let anything happen to you," he said soothingly.

By now, the sky was dark and low with ominous black clouds, the wind continuing to howl. As they pulled into the ranch's drive, a crack of lightning rent the air and, within seconds, the rolling boom of thunder reverberated directly overhead causing Frankie to shriek in alarm. Rain began to fall as if from buckets, cascading like waterfalls from heaven. The noise was deafening inside the truck and rain sheeted in front of them, drops hitting the vehicle as if they were bullets.

As they approached the last couple of hundred yards to the barn, lightning blindingly illuminated the whole area, an almighty clap of thunder reverberating instantaneously. To Frankie's horror, she watched as a horse bolted from the barn in a blind panic. Driven into a mad terror, it raced frantically toward the paddocks, attempting to escape the demons on its heels. Frankie gave a cry of fear as she recognized the horse as Delila.

She leapt from the truck, her clothes immediately drenched

as she ran after her horse. Rain blinded her eyes as she wildly looked around, endeavoring to locate the buckskin mare. She was only dimly aware of Luciano standing beside her in the downpour. Suddenly, he pointed frantically, fruitlessly yelling words she was helpless to hear. Giving up, he started to run toward the yards. Frankie followed, her progress made slippery by the rivers of water, mud threatening to suck off her boots. Her panicky breath rasped out of her as she battled onward.

"No," she whimpered in despair, as Luciano knelt down beside a mound that did not belong there. "No, no, no."

Delila raised her head as Frankie approached. Wire was wrapped around her hind legs, flesh stripped from her forelegs. Frankie kneeled.

"Steady, pretty girl," she crooned, looking at Luciano, the rain washing away her tears.

"Frankie, you need to keep her still. I have wire cutters in the truck. I'll be right back," he yelled over the roar of the storm. Frankie was barely able to make his words out.

It felt like an eternity for him to return and cut the wire from the mare's legs. Even longer to persuade Delila to stand and then slowly and painfully limp, slipping and sliding through the mud toward the barn. It was only after the broken mare was safely back in her stall that Frankie allowed herself to fully assess the damage.

Headlights shone through the rain and relief flooded through Frankie that her friends had returned safely from their own outing. Wild-eyed horror greeted the state of both Frankie and Luciano causing the girls to come running.

"Bloody heck," Megan uttered before turning and running for the first aid kit.

Deb stepped inside the stall, assessing the situation. "Luciano, we will need towels and some buckets of water." She looked to Frankie. "You okay, mate?" Frankie nodded mutely. "Gabi," Deb called. "You need to get the vet out here, ASAP."

It was much, much later by the time the vet left and Frankie crumpled gratefully into Luciano's arms. He'd remained with her the entire time, stoic in his support and assistance. Gabi paced beside them on the phone, agitatedly describing what had happened and seeking further expert advice.

"Carlos says that we are to send through the x-rays when they do them, but at this stage, he agrees with their early diagnosis. With the muscle damage and severed tendons in both hind legs, he said we can work on making her paddock sound, but Delila will never compete again." She looked sadly at Frankie. "I'm sorry, Frankie. She will never race again." Gabi rubbed at her red eyes, smearing the tears on her face.

Deb looked up from where she stood with Megan, drained from the evening's effort. "Both Megan and I have experience with this type of injury at the stud, and we're confident that, if we work with the vet, we can get her to be a sound broodmare." Megan nodded in agreement.

"Do you want us working with the vet from tonight or this Carlos?" Megan asked.

"For now, we work with the vet from tonight. But we run all the results and treatments past Carlos," Gabi answered, her voice rough with exhaustion. "Carlos is my brother. He's an equine vet, but he's in Kentucky doing some reproduction specialization training."

"At least she will live," Frankie said from the safe haven of Luc's arms. "She will hopefully have a long life of having future barrel racing babies."

All the friends nodded in agreement. "Here's to Delila, the Affinity Ranch Stud head studbook broodmare," Gabi said. She looked at Frankie forlornly. "I will have to call Black Angus tomorrow and let them know what happened. It will be a while before we hit the road again. We need to find a horse first."

"I have a horse," Frankie interjected. "Sampson."

"Look, Frankie, I know you think he could be a champion. But you don't know that yet. He's very unpredictable. Maybe it's best if we concentrate on getting you a going horse," Gabi argued.

"I think you should trust Frankie. If she thinks Sampson will make it, let her try," Megan said, rising in defense of her friend. "How long before you can get him seasoned enough to make a competitive time?"

Frankie tried not to get her hopes up as she considered. "He's still rough, but he's trying for me. Maybe a few more months at home and then haul to a few of the smaller events. The big thing will be how he handles the atmosphere." She paused. "That is, if you're happy with that plan as his owner." She raised questioning eyes to Luciano.

"We need to talk about this, Querida," he said softly. Frankie's heart dropped to her feet. "I do not think it is fair to either of you to put this pressure on Sampson."

Frankie blinked back the tears threatening to overflow. "I understand it is a chance," she implored. "But I know I can do it."

Luc's arms tightened around her. "Frankie, maybe you are right. If you are determined to do this, then I do not think I can do it as Sampson's owner. I bought him because I wanted you to have the chance you dreamed of. Maybe tonight has just sped that up. I will sign him over to you."

"What? Really?" The tears that had threatened now flowed freely down Frankie's cheeks. "I don't know what to say."

"You thank the man," Deb instructed gruffly.

Frankie turned in Luciano's embrace. Behind her, she heard Deb quietly usher the others upstairs. "Thank you, Luc. I don't think I can ever repay you for this."

"I did not do this for repayment. I did this because it made you happy. You are happy, Frankie?" Worried, he took in her sobbing features.

"Yes," she sniffled.

"Good. It was just hard to tell with all the tears."

"Maybe if you kiss me, the tears will stop," she suggested, lifting her face up to his.

"We can only try," he murmured, his lips grazing her ear.

CHAPTER 16

$\mathcal{D}$elila walked stiffly across her stall to accept the pieces of fresh grass Frankie held out for her. They had confined the mare to stall rest for the last two weeks, and she was profoundly over it. Frankie didn't have the heart to tell the stir-crazy horse that she still had at least another two months of it. Through the open doors at the end of the barn, she could make out Sampson digging up the dirt in readiness to roll. It figured, since she had only just finished giving him a wash at the end of his ride. Judging by all the wiggling and squirming, he had no intentions of cleanliness impeding a case of the itches.

"You sure you want to stay here with this lot?" asked Gabi, plonking herself against the wall beside Frankie. "Barretos is like nothing else. It's one heck of a party, and since Papai is still a big deal down there, we get to go to everything." Her face was comical in her over-enthusiasm. "And Luciano can show you off. Everyone wins." Gabi snapped her fingers as if she had just sealed the deal.

Frankie watched Delila delicately lip the last blade of grass off her hand before rubbing the dirt from her fingers. "Maybe next year. It does sound like fun. But right now, my head isn't in the right space to celebrate. I need to focus on getting Sampson going and ready to start hauling." She kept her eyes on the mare as she made painfully slow progress to the water bucket. "Plus, I wouldn't feel right leaving this one."

"Deb and Megan will still be here. They can look after her for the short time you will be gone." Both girls had declined the trip due to still having limited funds since moving. At this rate, the Barretos trip next year was going to be epic.

"I know, but I feel like I owe it to her to stay close to home until she is at least out of the stall," explained Frankie. "I swear, all I hear from both you and Luc is *Barretos*."

"Well Luciano loves Barretos. He's a celebrity back home. It's not like here, Frankie. The bull riders that have come over here and made it to the PBR—they are famous in Brazil."

"And I'm sure he will still be famous there next year," Frankie said. "Now, I need to rake the arena."

∼

In Barretos...

There was no other event in rodeo in the world that compared to Barretos. Energy sizzled around the grounds unlike any other event Luciano had ever competed in. Nothing could match it.

It was also the feeling of the familiar with friends that he had known since he was a boy coming to catch up on old times. His papai and mae never missed the festival. And after it was over, it was always hard to make himself leave again and head back to the States. This time, it was as if part of him was still in the States.

Frankie.

Luciano looked around until he caught sight of his father sitting at a table nursing a drink. His progress was slow as fans wanting pictures stopped him. He smiled ruefully and gave a helpless little shrug as he looked to Papai, waiting patiently. Finally, he made it and gave his father a warm hug, slapping him on the back in greeting.

Taking a seat, he looked the older man up and down approvingly. "Papai, I see Mae is still filling your bowl up for you."

Papai rubbed his belly, laughing. "It's how I know how much your Mae loves me. And by eating it all, I show her how much I love her back."

"You both must love each other a lot then." Luciano roared with laughter.

His father rubbed his belly again, chortling. "Lots. But how are you feeling? Will this be your Barretos?"

Luciano's face grew grave, his eyes filled with steely determination. "This time, I feel in my bones, is my time."

Papai reached over and slapped his son on the shoulder in approval. "I believe you. There is something different about you. More focused."

"It is my time, Papai, for everything. You should see the ranch. I am putting in some new fencing now and fixing up the machinery shed. Frankie will need a new arena for training, too. And I'm feeling strong, Papai, riding well." Steely resolve radiated from him as he spoke.

"Mae and I cannot wait to see your ranch. And meet this Frankie?" His sentence ended with a questioning note in his voice.

Luciano's expression softened at the mention of her name. "Papai, you used to tell me that, one day, I would meet a woman, and all the other women would just fade into the background as if they never existed. That I would know"—he thumped his chest above his heart—"here." A silly grin broke out over his face, the corners of his eyes crinkling. "Now I know this to be true. There is only Frankie for me."

His father beamed his happy approval at him, once again

thumping him on the arm. "I can't wait to meet my future daughter-in-law. This calls for another drink." He signaled a passing waiter.

"Nothing for me, Papai. I need to start getting ready to ride." Luciano moved to stand.

"Excuse me, are you Luciano Navarro?" a light feminine voice interrupted. Luciano turned to see a voluptuous young woman, her eyes boldly appraising him. Behind her, a group of what appeared to be her friends stood in a giggling little group.

"Yes, I am."

She took a deep breath, her breasts threatening to spill from her low-cut tank top. "I am your biggest fan," she said, her guileless eyes wide in admiration as she brought her palm to rest on her amply displayed assets. "Can I get a picture with you?"

Luciano smiled at her. "You sure can."

The bulls had fought hard, but Luciano had ridden harder to emerge as the champion of Barretos. All around him, his friends and family celebrated as the alcohol flowed and the music pulsed its rhythmic beat. In the crowd, he could see Joao coming in and out of focus as he shyly talked to Gabi, Senhor Eduardo close at hand as chaperone, catching up with acquaintances. Papai exuberantly twirled Mae about the dance floor, giddy in their son's win and the reflected glory after hard years of toiling. The room tilted slightly, making Luciano grip his beer bottle tighter.

The only thing missing was Frankie. He had called her as soon as he had walked off the arena, the sand still clinging to his chaps, the roar of the crowd's approval still ringing in his ears. Her sweet voice on the other end as she congratulated him had almost brought him to his knees, longing for her to share in this particular moment overwhelming him. Soon, he promised himself. Soon, she would always be by his side for moments like this, as he would be by hers.

Feeling the pressing desire to relieve his bladder, he staggered outside. A slight breeze whispered across his sweat-drenched face as he raised his hat to wipe his brow. He leaned one hand against the wall and closed his eyes in ecstasy as the pressure drained away. His need taken care of, he staggered back to the party.

Emerging from the shadows, the voluptuous fan from earlier appeared, phone in hand. She handed it to her friend still shrouded by the darkness. "Make sure you get everything," she commanded before stalking after her prey.

CHAPTER 17

*D*read's icy fingers trailed over Frankie, leaving spasms of wretchedness in its wake. As the blood drained from her extremities, it left behind a curious sense of numbness, an inability to release her hold. A hold that still gripped the phone tightly. A phone she now felt helpless to look away from.

Three images had shown up on her media feed, Luciano having been tagged with the caption *My champion*. The first had been innocuous enough. A voluptuous, what appeared to be Brazilian girl cozying up to Luc for a fan photo, the sun shining brightly behind them. The next was less innocent. It appeared to have been taken at night and showed the same girl, but this time, her tight top was pulled dangerously low and her head was tipped back in laughter as she caressed a drunkenly smiling Luciano's arm. But it was the final one that shattered Frankie's heart into a million pieces. The same girl now leaned in, smiling coyly as Luciano whispered into her ear.

Megan breezed into the feed room, barely visible over the buckets that were piled high in the wheelbarrow she pushed. "I wonder if Gabi is getting sick of all of her family asking when she is going to meet a nice boy." Megan laughed. She was probably imagining Gabi stuck for an extra week with her extended Brazilian family. Blind to the emotional turmoil that still held Frankie fast, she blithely ploughed on. "At least Luc was smart enough to go, get the job done, and come home. It's today he comes home, isn't it? You must be excited." When no response came, she peered curiously around at Frankie. Observing her chalky complexion, concern creased her face. "Are you okay, Frankie?"

A mute Frankie robotically held the phone out to her friend. Megan glanced down, her brows furrowing together as she perused the images before looking at Frankie in horrified surprise, her mouth agape.

"What the heck, Frankie?" she exclaimed. "Who the heck is that skank?"

Frankie shook her head miserably and shrugged. "I have no idea."

"Strewth, what the heck happened in Brazil?" Megan's eyes were still wide in disbelief.

"I think that's pretty obvious."

Megan looked down at the phone again. "Um, maybe you need to speak to Luciano and find out what's going on," she suggested.

"No. I should have known it was just a game to someone like him." The anguish welled up inside her, catching the words in her throat.

Megan looked at her friend in despair, and Frankie hunched over, swallowing back a sob. Megan took her in her arms, holding her tight as Frankie's body shuddered with the force of her tears. "Gosh dang men," Megan said as though filled with an icy blast of incandescent rage. "Give me horses any day. If they jump the fence too often, at least it's legal to geld them!"

～

The hard bite of wood as the stall door hit her side made Frankie cry out in pain. She winced, gingerly touching her ribs, and she bit down, determined not to allow the tears that threatened to flow. It felt like that was all she had done in the hours since she had seen the images of Luciano's betrayal, now seared into her mind as surely as if he had held the branding iron himself.

To her fevered imagination, it was as if she had somehow magically conjured him up. Echoing footsteps announced his presence long before his rugged profile materialized from the outside darkness. Frankie's heart pounded in her chest as his familiar swaggering stride brought him closer, the crunch of the gravel embedded in the soles of his boots unnaturally loud in the otherwise deathly silence.

She once again saw him whispering into the girl's ear in her mind's eye. Frankie bit down hard on her lip, the sharp metallic taste of blood a welcome distraction from the torturous burden of anguish she carried inside. Watching his approach, she hugged herself, gripping her elbows tightly.

"He has some nerve coming here." Deb mutinously glared as she and Megan stepped from neighboring stalls to stand protectively beside Frankie, watching his approach.

It was all still too raw for Frankie, her heart still fractured, once again on the brink of tears. Then, he smiled that dang smile of his, and she felt something snap inside her. The 180-degree change in emotion was momentarily disorientating.

The white-hot burn of anger filled her as she turned, nostrils flared, to her friends. "It's okay, you guys can go. There are some things I want to say to him."

Megan shoved her hands in her pockets as she looked doubtfully at Deb. Deb opened her mouth as if to protest before closing it and giving a sharp nod.

"Just remember, if you need us, give a yell, and we will give him what for," she whispered, her eyes gleaming at the prospect of giving the lothario a piece of her mind. Frankie nodded back with a sad little smile.

"Good evening, ladies." Luciano, the very embodiment of male confidence, sauntered closer. Both girls shot him daggers before turning on their heels and heading for the feed room. Luciano scratched his chin, confusion easily read on his face. "Was it something I said? But no mind, I have missed you, Querida." He reached to embrace Frankie.

She recoiled back, pressing herself against the rough timber stall wall. "Don't touch me," she ground out through clenched teeth. "And don't you dare call me Querida."

Luciano's face crumpled in hurt bafflement. "What is going on, Frankie?"

The final strand of her nerves snapped, unraveling her control even as she fought to stitch it back in place. "Really?" hissed Frankie. "*Really*? That's how you wanna play this?" Disgust made her wrinkle her nose as she angrily dug in her pocket for her phone. Her movements sharp, she brought the images up before she thrust it into Luciano's hand. "You don't get to do that after this."

He lowered his head, peering at the screen. He jerked back in astonishment and leveled a look back at her. "What are these?"

"Are you for real right now? Did you really think that chick wouldn't post those all over the internet? Look, if you were tired of me, you should have been a man and had the decency to break up with me. I deserved that respect at least."

"I don't want to break up with you," he refuted sharply. "I don't know what these photos are."

"Give me more credit than that," snarled Frankie. "Maybe you didn't want to break up with me, but that didn't stop you from going back home and having some fun chasing tail while you were there."

Frankie's steely armor of resolve weakened at the hurt look Luciano leveled at her. "Frankie, I am famous there.

Women, they throw themselves at me and before, I'd take my pick of them all." Frankie's face crumpled at the words he threw at her. He leaned in closer until his face was level with hers. "But that was before you. This first photo"—he stabbed his finger at the screen for emphasis—"I took. You can see my papai in the background. I remember her asking to take it. The last two were after I won, I think." His brow was furrowed, like he was searching his memories. "I was celebrating. And yes, I drank too much, and there were lots of people there. I don't remember her. I know I woke up in my own bed, alone. How quickly your feelings have turned to hate for me. Did you even fight it? Or was it easier to just give in and think that I am a man that would do that? I have done nothing wrong. If you really knew me like I thought you did, Frankie, you wouldn't doubt it."

He gave her one last lingering look, his face a hostile mask of rage and hurt. But worse were his eyes, those beautiful, laughing eyes now a well of betrayal and pain. He turned and, without looking back, walked away.

"Goodbye, Frankie."

CHAPTER 18

"Okay, what have I missed?" Gabi perched on the kitchen counter, coffee mug in hand. She had arrived home in the early hours of the morning and only now emerged from her room in the late afternoon. She smiled impishly. "Bet you gave Luciano a champion's welcome when he got home?"

Bedlam greeted her innocent question with Deb frantically giving her a cutting-off gesture, slashing her fingers near her throat. Simultaneously, Megan choked on her sip of coffee, spluttering furiously for air. Deb stopped her wild gesturing to thump her friend on her back, all the while shooting concerned looks at Frankie who had remained strangely composed through the ordeal, staring blankly into her coffee mug.

Gabi looked wide-eyed at the madhouse she suddenly found herself in. "Ah," she began hesitantly. "I feel like maybe I need to proceed with caution, but for the life of me, I can't figure out why."

Megan and Deb darted an apprehensive look between them.

Frankie sighed dejectedly. "It's all right, guys. I won't shatter from telling her what happened."

Gabi's brow wrinkled in alarm. "Guys, what the heck happened?"

"We broke up."

"What? Why?" Surprise shot across Gabi's face, her hand flying to her chest in alarm.

"Just show her the photos," Frankie softly commanded, not raising her eyes from her drink.

Deb grabbed her phone from the counter and tapped at it quickly. Gabi curiously peered down at the screen. "I think these look a lot worse than they are," she began tentatively, swirling her coffee. "I think they could be … misinterpreted."

"How could him being all over her be misinterpreted?" cried Frankie in disbelief at her friend's betrayal.

Gabi glanced down at her now cold cup of coffee. "I think maybe this all needs to be explained over a drink."

The smoke added to the already gloomy interior of The Wonky Cowboy, gathering fog like beneath the dim lights. The steady hum of humanity trying to compete with the jukebox made any semblance of a conversation an exercise in futility. The bar was packed to the rafters, the perfect combination of it being Friday night and the influx of spectators and competitors for the local rodeo. Everyone there looked just a little too happy, Frankie thought sourly as she waited to grab a drink at the bar.

"Hi, gorgeous," drawled the blond guy waiting beside her as he looked her up and down appreciatively.

"Oh, hi," she said absently, leaning forward to tell her order to the barman.

"Are you from around here?" he asked, clearly not getting the hint.

"What, um, yeah?"

"I'm here for the rodeo. Bronc rider. Maybe I can get you in for free or something."

"I think I can manage." She grabbed her drinks. As she brushed past him, his hand took a swipe at her arse causing her to stiffen. "Mate, tonight is not the night to mess with me," she threatened before making her way over to her friends.

"Who was that?" Deb peered across the crowd to where the bronc-riding arse-grabber was still propping himself up by the bar. "He's kinda cute."

"And handsy," Frankie sourly noted as she handed the drinks out.

"Frankie, we need to get this Luciano stuff all straightened out," began Gabi. "I was there, I'm sure from a different angle I could be in those pics in the background."

"I don't really want to think about this anymore. I'm done crying. I'm tired of feeling confused about how he feels—felt. Gosh, I'm not even sure if he felt the same way I did. How do I know what I was feeling was even real? I'm sick of feeling like my head is all over the place." Frankie laughed a little too loudly. "I just have little experience with guys, and whenever I think maybe I know what to expect, it turns out I know nothing at all."

Gabi captured the other girl's wrists. "You need to listen to me. Nothing. Happened." She enunciated the words. "I don't care what those picture show. Whenever anyone went near Luciano that night, all he could talk about was his beautiful Australian Querida. To be honest, it started out cute but was getting annoying by the end of the night."

"Then why is this chick all over him?" Frankie blurted, the words explosively flying from her mouth propelled by her hurt.

"Frankie, understand that, back in Brazil, he is very famous. Women will always throw themselves at him. Maybe he could have handled it better, but he was very drunk and still all he could think about was you."

Doubt began to worm itself past Frankie's determined armor. She bit her lip uncertainly. "I don't know. I'm so confused."

"Frankie, there is nothing to be confused about. He loves you. He gave you Sampson for gosh sake. When a cowboy gives his heart, he gives it all. You need to trust him. I saw him leave with my own eyes with his papai and mae. *Alone.*" She said firmly, her eyes drilling ruthlessly into Frankie's.

Frankie's eyes darkened with doubt, her expression troubled. "Maybe I was wrong." Uncertainty shaded her words.

Gabi gave her hands a reassuring squeeze. "I think you are, honey. For what it's worth, he loves you, so he will probably forgive you."

"What if he doesn't?"

"Then we'll figure out what to do then. But I think when he calms down, you guys will be able to work it out."

Frankie's mind reeled with her friend's revelations. "I think I need some fresh air."

The fresh night air was a welcome relief after the cancer-inducing atmosphere of the bar. Frankie breathed in deeply, the ramification of Gabi's words hitting her like a sledgehammer.

"What have I done?" she whispered miserably.

"What was that, darlin'?" a slightly familiar voice asked, slipping an arm around her shoulders.

Oh, great, she thought. The arse-grabber from the bar had followed her out. She shrugged his arm off, stepping away from him in revulsion. "Mate, you need to stop with all the touching."

"I just thought we could become a little friendlier." He stepped into her space again. Frankie's scalp prickled at his nearness, unease trickling up her spine.

"Mate, back off," she commanded, her eyes narrowing in warning.

"I like them a little feisty." He leered at her, leaving her skin crawling at his closeness.

"You need to listen to her," a sweetly familiar voice growled from behind. Frankie's muscles went weak as relief coursed through her. Luciano's hand was firm on her shoulder as he possessively pulled her close. "She is already taken. But if you were a true cowboy, you would respect her saying no, regardless."

"Whatever," her assailant muttered. "There's plenty of other tail in the bar anyway."

Frankie watched in delight as he walked away, conscious of the tension radiating from Luciano as he followed the other man with his eyes. "Um, thank you, Luc. I guess I was lucky you came along. But I was dealing with it," she said, awkwardly defensive, self-conscious now the threat had passed.

He made no move to release his hold on her. He lowered his head to her hair for a moment to breathe in deeply. "No matter how angry I am with you, Querida, I will always protect you." She felt his lips smile. "I am sure he does not know how lucky he was that I didn't leave you to deal with him."

He released his hold on her and moved back a pace, his expression guarded once again. Frankie felt suddenly bereft at the loss of his warm closeness, unsure of how to return things to how they were. Raucous laughter broke the tension as a drunkenly, amorous couple staggered out from the bar.

Sharp clarity transcended over Frankie. Regardless of what she thought she had seen, she should never have doubted him. Deep down, she knew she could trust him. She felt sick with remorse at the havoc she had wreaked on her relationship with this steadfast cowboy. She could only pray now that she could somehow mend the damage.

"Luc, I think I was wrong about. You know, the photos," she fumbled over her words.

An odd shadow flickered through his eyes. "Frankie, you needed to trust me," he said shortly.

A cold ball of despair built in Frankie's belly. "I know. And I'm sorry." Her voice caught, thick with tears. "I just have some insecurities, I guess, about if someone wants to be with me." She swallowed down her sorrow. "That shouldn't be an excuse, but I'm trying to explain why I reacted the way I did."

"Frankie, I am sorry you have been hurt, but I am not that person," he said gruffly, still not looking her in the eye.

"I know, Luc. I know I was wrong, and I want whatever we had again," she pleaded softly. "I miss you."

Luciano finally looked at her, tilting her chin up gently with his hand. "Do you really not know what we have, Querida?"

Frankie tried to look away from his intense gaze, but he wouldn't let her. "I, ah, know we like each other."

Luciano gave a hollow laugh. "I think it is time I say goodnight, Frankie. I hope to see you tomorrow night."

The cold ball of despair hardened in her belly until it turned to lead. She watched helplessly as he walked away, the tears sliding unchecked down her cheeks. When he disappeared from view, her legs crumbled beneath her, no longer able to hold her weight. On the dirty sidewalk, among the stumbling drunks, she wailed her pain out to the night.

CHAPTER 19

Gabi and Megan sniffed the air with relish. The prospect of the food vans had both girls excitedly forging ahead, eager to sample the culinary delights the various aromas wafting gently on the breeze promised. Frankie scuffed her boots in the dirt, dragging her feet slowly behind them, too caught up in her misery to be tempted by the prospect. The last place she felt like being tonight was here. The very idea of seeing Luciano after last night felt as appealing as pouring vinegar on a grazed knee. Frankie was too emotionally raw to be able to handle the likelihood of running into him with aplomb.

"Come on, Frankie," Megan called back, attempting to hurry her along. "You look about as happy as a cat in a room full of rocking chairs."

"Why is there a room full of rocking chairs?" Gabi looked baffled. "Like, in an old people's home or something?"

"It's just a saying. You know the cat wouldn't be thrilled with all those chairs trying to squish its tail," Megan explained, her attention still firmly fixed on her prospective meals.

"Maybe the cat doesn't have a tail. You know, like one of those Manx cats," Gabi suggested.

"I think you are missing the point, Gabi. Frankie looks about as happy as Deb did this morning doing the walk of shame home."

"In all fairness, Deb looked happy with herself. She was just incredibly hungover." Gabi grimaced in sympathy at the memory.

"Yeah, she said he showed her a good time, but they were both drunk when they left." Megan gave a little giggle. "I'm not sure he could even show her an okay time."

"True that." Gabi joined in the giggling. "Speaking of which, I've decided I want a corn dog."

"I might get one too. The way we've been going, it's probably the closest we'll get to a wiener."

Frankie let her friends' banter flow around her, not having the heart to partake in the easy jesting. As she followed them, she made a mental note to be more forceful in her refusal the next time they bullied her into coming along to something she didn't feel like doing. The dying moose noises Deb had been making when they left were preferable to this.

She aimlessly trailed behind, not paying particular attention until she realized she had been separated from them. Not only that, but she had stumbled on the entrance of the competitors' area. Realizing her mistake, she turned to make a hasty retreat.

"I don't care what your boyfriend said last night. I think you want it," a horribly familiar voice taunted. The arse-grabber from the previous night blocked her escape. "And I'm more than happy to give it to you."

Frankie rolled her eyes heavenward. *Great, just what I need right now.* "Give up already," she said in a frustrated voice.

"Oh, I'll give it up all right," he said, leaving Frankie feeling like she desperately needed a hot shower with a whole heap of soap, probably disinfectant at the very least. "I'm gonna put it up in places you never—"

With a startled bellow, he fell backward, sprawled at Luciano's feet. Frankie stared incredulously as he lay for a moment, making gasping noises before he recovered and leapt to his feet.

Luciano stared at him, nostrils flared, menace radiating from every pore. "I warned you last night."

"The lady is hot for it. Maybe you don't do it for her anymore," the arse-grabber sneered, impervious to the imminent threat of peril to his person.

Luciano stood, skin mottled with rage, the tendons in his neck corded, the wrath within fighting against the constraint of his skin. A guttural roar tore from his very soul. Teeth bared, he lowered his head as he barreled toward his tormentor.

The force of his assault sent both men flying to the ground. The bronc rider had fistfuls of Luciano's clothing as he attempted to wrestle himself from underneath, flailing like a fish on land. Frankie jumped clear of the melee, looking around for help.

Luciano used his greater size to his advantage, raining blows down, his rampage escalating. The crack of knuckles striking bone reverberated, making Frankie wince. And still, Luciano did not cease. His nemesis no longer looked to join the battle but was, instead, desperately seeking an escape from the pain that pulsated through his body and the one that inflicted it. Just as Frankie feared that Luciano would kill the bronc rider, Joao materialized, dragging Luciano clear.

Luciano flexed his hand experimentally, blood on his knuckles as he looked down in disdain at the vanquished cowboy, gingerly trying to right himself. "You stay away from her. If you don't, next time my friend won't be around to stop me from really teaching you manners. I will destroy any hope you have of making it in rodeo. You know who I am. You are no one. I will make sure no one will sponsor you, that any events you enter will already be full. Stay away."

Luciano spat at the ground beside his fallen foe. His rival stared up at him with hostile, hate-filled eyes that were already swollen into tight slits. Blood seeped crimson from his bent nose and split lip.

Luciano strode away from him with Joao on his heels. As he neared Frankie, he firmly took her upper arm in his grasp. "You and I will have a little talk." His tone brooked no argument. Frankie meekly complied, cowed by the display she had witnessed.

After walking a short distance, Luciano abruptly stopped, speaking rapidly to Joao before clasping his hand in what appeared to be thanks. Joao nodded as he left. He gave Frankie an encouraging smile—one she chose to interpret as support. Luciano turned his commanding gaze to her.

"I think you cannot stay out of trouble."

"That's not fair," she protested, stung at his comment. "You have known me how long? And how often has it happened?"

"Twice in the last two nights." He held up two battle-damaged fingers to emphasize his point.

Frankie crossed her arms defensively over her chest. "I did nothing to encourage him," she declared. "Why would I? I'm having enough problems with you, and I love you!" she shouted, her eyes opening wide in horror at what she had inadvertently blurted out.

A slow, smug smile crept over Luciano's face till the familiar lines creased his face. "I wondered how long it would take you to figure it out."

A dull flush crept along Frankie's cheeks as embarrassed tears welled. She scrubbed at her eyes in angry frustration at their betrayal. Work-roughened hands that had caused blood to flow in her defense only moments earlier now gently lowered hers from her face before pulling her into his arms. *Home.* It finally dawned on Frankie. *It feels like home.*

"When I first saw you, it was as if my heart already knew." His voice rumbled in his chest against Frankie's ear. "But I did not think you were ready to hear it. I thought maybe, if I tell you I love you, you would run away scared."

Frankie sniffled into his chest. "I think maybe I knew. Well, I knew there was something there. It was like you completed the missing pieces that I didn't even know I had. It scared me."

"Querida, how I feel about you, it scares me too. But it feels right. The last few days, I never want to do again."

Frankie raised her head from his chest and looked at him, her eyes shining brightly through her tears. "Me neither. I love you, Luc."

"I love you, too, Querida." He lowered his head, his lips commanding on hers as he laid claim to what was his.

It proved to be a successful night all round. Luciano won the buckle, both Megan and Gabi ate their fill, and a cowboy finally got his cowgirl.

CHAPTER 20

*T*he weeks flew by, as time is wont to do, ever relentless in its rhythm. Gabi scoured the country-side looking for mares suitable to add to their breeding program, all the while juggling the business. She secured a deal with a local stud to have their colts sent to Frankie for training. The stud owners, having seen her ride at Need for Speed, were keen to get their horses in for training early, confident her star would rise.

Megan and Deb had their hands full with the influx of horses coming in. Delila had been granted permission from Gabi's brother, Carlos, to leave the confines of her stall to the relative freedom of a small yard. All the while, Sampson continued to improve under Frankie's tutelage. Luciano, now staring down the barrel of having qualified for the NFR, was away most weekends, and Frankie's workload only allowed her to attend some of his events in support.

Frankie was never sure what the near future would bring, only able to focus on one day at a time. It was fair to say, without Gabi's firm hand at the helm, she would have felt battered by the storm of life. Each morning, Sampson took priority and was worked before she moved on to whichever outside colts were in for training or sale. By early afternoon, after she had handed the last horse over to be cooled down, she would head inside.

Settling down to paperwork, she would work through training notes to send to clients, plan any events they might need to get hauled to and arrange times for potential buyers to inspect them. Late afternoon found her catching up with Gabi to find out what the next day would bring.

Frankie sunk gratefully into her chair, exhaustion's shadow upon her face. "That roan colt should sell tomorrow, if the buyers are genuine. He's turned out to be a real sweetheart," she said, rubbing her tired eyes.

Gabi looked up from her spreadsheet. "The owners will be happy. How many is that this month?" she asked rhetorically, consulting her computer. "That's five you've sold for them this month."

"Just trying to keep the client happy." Frankie absently rubbed her neck. "Sampson is almost ready to haul to some small events, too."

Gabi looked up, a keen interest in her eyes. "How long before you know if he will be able to step up to bigger events?" she said, leaning forward on her elbows. "Black Angus have been patient, but we need you out there again getting your name about."

Frankie looked down at her hands, considering the question. "The first few events will be a big indicator. He's improving his runs all the time at home, but it just depends on how he handles the atmosphere once we're out."

"Carlos is going to visit soon. I'll get him to give Delila the once over in the flesh. If he's happy, we'll look at putting her to Sampson. That should produce one heck of a foal." Gabi's dark eyes flashed happily at the thought of the match.

"I'm too young to be a grandmother," Frankie joked, stifling a yawn. "I better have a shower and get going." She rose wearily to her feet. "No rest for the wicked."

"You love it." Gabi chuckled. "Speaking of wicked—or should I say, wicked thoughts—say hello to Luciano for me and wish him luck for the weekend."

"Will do. He's so focused right now. If he can manage to not have any injuries, he has a good chance at the finals in Vegas." She yawned again. "Anyway, better keep moving."

~

Frankie sat, drowsy with contentment, empty plate before her mute evidence to the vigor of her hunger. Across the table, she watched Luciano scrape up the last of the mashed potato that had accompanied the already-inhaled T-bone. He gave a satisfied groan of overindulgence as he smacked his lips, the final morsel having melted away in his mouth. Catching her indulgent smile, he raised an eyebrow comically.

"That I enjoyed." He belched. "Maybe a little too much." The corners of his mouth twitched.

An ache filled her. Suddenly, it felt as if he was too far away from her. The need to be physically close to him made her slide her foot under the table until her leg settled against his. Luciano's dark eyes glowed warmly at her.

"I like that you no longer hide that you want to touch me."

Frankie gave him a playful smile. "I like it, too." A whisper of a thought entered her mind. "Everything about you makes me feel warm and safe. I didn't expect that," she said.

He leaned forward to capture her hands in his, rubbing his thumbs in a circular motion on the back. The friction from the rough pad of his thumbs sent waves of electricity shooting through Frankie. "I love this is how I make you feel, Querida. But I hope that is not all you feel when I touch you."

It was impossible for her not to be captivated by his magnetism as he stared intently into her eyes, a promise evident in his gaze.

She gave a breathless little laugh, her mouth suddenly dry. She wet her lips with the tip of her tongue. "You are a very tempting man, Luc."

His gaze was hot as he stared at her mouth, unable to look away. "You will get us into trouble if you keep doing that," he growled.

A feeling of power surged through Frankie. Never in a million years had she thought she could attract the attention of a man like Luciano. But not only had she captured it, she also held it, along with his heart. Happiness blazed from her shining eyes as she looked at her cowboy.

"I think it might be time to ask for the check."

CHAPTER 21

The light show flashed as the rodeo queens galloped their horses in an intricately choreographed display, flags flying behind them. Frankie perched on the edge of her seat, excited as a kid on Christmas morning. She had seen footage of the previous years' events, but to actually sit in the hallowed space that was the Thomas and Mack Arena exceeded even her wildest dreams. She felt a twinge of pity that Megan and Deb had had to stay behind to manage the stud.

The queens disappeared out of the arena as the spotlight once again focused, its bright lights heralding the beginning of the next event—bull riding. An expectant quiet fell over the crowd as the announcer began his preamble of what was to come. The tension grew as he finally began to introduce the bull riders, fire flowing like lava across the surface of the arena as they walked one by one through a blizzard of fireworks.

"Oh my gosh, there he is!" squealed Gabi beside her as Luciano stepped proudly through the sparks.

Frankie filled her eyes with the glorious sight of Luciano, magnetic strength resonating from him as he stood with his fellow competitors. Soon, the showdown would begin in earnest. But for now, each stood to savor the moment as if to last a lifetime. She turned to Gabi, her eyes shiny with excitement.

"He looks good, doesn't he?"

Her friend nodded enthusiastically. "Like a champion." Gabi scanned the other bull riders. "Joao looks like he means business too."

Frankie looked at her in surprise. It wasn't like her to actually notice Joao, more like him always noticing her. "Yes, he does. Luc says he has shown a lot of improvement this year." The main lights flooded the arena causing the girls to settle back into their chairs. "Showtime."

As eight seconds flashed up on the clock, both girls hugged each other, giving a little squeal.

"That was a good ride, right?" Frankie looked to Gabi for affirmation. "He'll score well with that, don't you think?"

Gabi laughed. "Do I get a chance to answer or would you just like to rapid-fire questions at me?" she teased her friend, giving her a nudge with her shoulder. "I think he rode well, but we will find out any minute now."

Both girls watched the big screen with bated breath. Frankie let out a long sigh as 88 materialized on the screen. "Ladies and gentlemen, the big Brazilian has done enough to be the round winner for tonight. Put your hands together and make some noise."

Frankie smiled proudly. "Guess we better congratulate tonight's winner."

"I guess. Hey Frankie, how did he know?" Gabi asked curiously.

"Know what?" Frankie confused, gathered up her coat.

"That he's big."

Frankie threw her coat at Gabi in mock disgust. "Really? That's the angle you want to go with?"

"Well, is there an angle you prefer, or is that strictly between you and Luc?"

Frankie threw her hands up in despair. "I give up. You're starting to sound like Deb."

∽

The South Point presentation room was packed to overflowing for the go round winners buckle presentation. It wasn't much better backstage as all the winners had their posse of family, friends and supporters ready to amble on stage when it was their turn.

Frankie stood soaking in the triumphant atmosphere, secure with Luc's arm wrapped snuggly around her waist as people congratulated him. Though the air was jubilant, a sense of anticipation still hung. A win in the round was a great achievement and step in the right direction, but it still wasn't the ultimate prize every competitor came to the NFR for. Frankie craned her neck to see a glimpse of the stage as the roping winner stepped out with supporters in tow.

Senhor Eduardo stood beside them with Gabi and Joao, his expression far away as if lost in memories of rodeo championships gone by. Frankie wondered if an old bull rider ever lost the urge to prove they were the best, the one to tame the beast for eight seconds. From the stage, the banter of the hosts continued as they included the VIPs and Rodeo Queens in the presentation.

"Ladies and gentlemen, once again, put your hands together for tonight's roping round champion, Colt McGomery, and keep them together as we welcome to the stage the Rampaging Brazilian, tonight's go round bull riding winner, Luciano Navarro."

Luciano gently took Frankie by the elbow and guided her

out onto the stage. The bright glare of the spotlights momentarily blinded her before her eyes adjusted and she looked out into a sea of rapt faces.

"Luciano, would you like to introduce who you have up here tonight?" the host asked.

"This is my Frankie, my girlfriend. The great Senhor Eduardo Cabrera, and his daughter and Frankie's business partner, Gabriella, and my good friend and competitor, Joao Rojas," Luciano said as he introduced them down the line.

The babble of conversation between the host and Luc swirled around Frankie, his magnetic personality out in full force as he had the crowd eating out of his hand. It was easy to see why they loved him. Frankie knew they only glimpsed a part of him, the bright, shiny Luciano, the champion.

She perceived all of him, the heart of the man, and knew she was the real winner. The glamorous Rodeo Queen came on stage to present the boxed winner's presentation buckle, and everyone gathered in close for a photo. Before she was aware of it, they were walking off stage and headed to the bar to get a celebratory drink. She excused herself to head to the bathroom, and Gabi elected to accompany her.

"What a rush." Gabi bounced on the balls of her feet, the adrenaline still coursing through her system. "It will be us up there one day soon." Her face was serious. "I mean that, Frankie. I really believe we can do it."

Frankie looked at her reflection in the mirror, seeing a slight blonde girl with a smattering of freckles across her nose. The girl looking back at her had a fire in her eyes that previously burned inside her, hidden away. She caught her friend's eye in the mirror.

"I believe we can, too. But for now, I'm happy to go celebrate with my champion."

The friends had to fight their way through the crowd to find the others. As they got closer, a slender brunette in a tight-fitting dress and a push-up bra draped herself over

Luciano. A hot flash of anger sizzled through Frankie as the woman whispered in his ear. Luciano shrugged her off, taking a step away to create space between them.

"Gosh, some women have no shame," Gabi muttered in disgust.

"Here, hold my drink," ordered Frankie, stalking toward the pair.

"Christ, this should be interesting," Gabi said, hurrying after her.

The buxom buckle bunny gave Frankie a sullen look as she approached, clearly recognizing her from the stage. She made a step to sidle closer to Luciano but was thwarted by him turning and presenting her with his back as he reached for Frankie.

Frankie gave him a tight smile as she stepped around him to his would-be suitor. She gave her a hard look, scrutinizing her from head to toe.

"Look, mate, but did you not hear him say up there"— Frankie gestured over her shoulder to the stage—"I am his Frankie, his *girlfriend*. He doesn't have time for skanks like you, so rack off." The skank in question gave a huff and strutted off, her nose in the air.

Luciano's eyes glowed with approval, and her heart sung as he gave her a slow, sexy smile. "Well, my kitten has claws."

"Someone had to take the trash out. And they all need to realize that you are mine and I don't share." She raised her chin defiantly, daring him to make fun of her.

He caught her in a bone-crushing hug, his solid warmth feeling like home. "I love you, my Querida."

CHAPTER 22

Frankie's eyes were agog at the press of humanity that flowed down the broad avenue of Cowboy Christmas. She was amazed at the variety of techniques the savvy shoppers employed. Some flitted from stall to stall like butterflies fluttering from one shopping flower to another, ever relentless in their quest for bargains. And others ambled about, ever consistent in their steady perusal of merchandise. Frankie couldn't remember when she had last enjoyed people watching so much. There was something verging on magical about being one of the crowd.

The Black Angus setup had seen a considerable volume of people visiting their display as the public came to get an autograph and photo with whom many considered the likely soon-to-be-crowned world bull riding champion.

Luciano was his usual affable, charismatic self, enjoying the adoration shining at him. Frankie shifted a little in her seat beside him. Although she was technically there in her role as a sponsored rider, it was clear whom everyone wanted to see. She watched as a little cowgirl wove her way in and out of the crowd as she held tightly onto her father's hand, her braids bouncing with each impatient step. The girl was on a mission and wasn't letting anyone slow her pink cowboy boot strides down. It was with some surprise, Frankie realized, she was headed toward their table.

Assuming they would attach themselves to the end of Luciano's rather lengthy queue, Frankie was astonished when the girl blithely skipped up to position herself in front of her.

"Hiya, how are you doing?" she greeted her small visitor.

"Ima doing fine," she mumbled shyly as she looked up at Frankie through long black eyelashes.

"You're all I've heard about since she found out you'd be here and now she is quiet as a clam." Her father rested his hand fondly on his daughter's head for a moment. "Would you like a photo with Frankie Smith?" he asked, smiling indulgently.

The little moppet nodded her head vigorously, her eyes shining bright. Luciano looked up from signing another autograph. "Looks like you have yourself a number one fan."

The little girl smiled at him shyly. "My daddy thinks you're a good bull wider, even if you aren't fwom here." Her father coughed uncomfortably, looking away embarrassedly.

Frankie laughed, looking at Luciano in amusement. "Well, is that so? Maybe we should all get a photo?" she suggested.

The little girl looked up at her father excitedly for approval. "That would be great, if these other people wouldn't mind." He glanced at the long line of waiting fans.

Luciano turned his megawatt smile up to full force. "I'm sure they won't mind making a little girl happy."

As they gathered for the photo, Frankie was caught by surprise at the little pang of longing she felt as she knelt and put her arms around the tiny cowgirl. Maybe one day she would have one of her own, one with dark laughing eyes. She looked at Luciano, wondering what their child would look like. He caught her speculative expression and sent her a questioning look in return, eyebrow raised. She smiled at him enigmatically before returning her attention to the little girl.

"Have you found anything that you like here?" she asked curiously.

Her father laughed. "Only if it was a buckskin mare called Delila. I took her to Need for Speed to see her cousin's race, and she saw the two of you win. Since then, all she wants to do is ride like Frankie and Delila. It's been a rough time for her." His eyes clouded briefly. "So, I'm grateful that she has had you, so to speak."

Frankie wondered at the pain in the man's words. "Well, Delila is out in a paddock, and hopefully next year, she will have a little black or buckskin foal. Maybe you could help us come up with a name when it comes."

The little girl's expression became solemn as she gravely pondered her new responsibility. "Daddy will have to send you an email, 'cwause I'm not allowed to."

"I'm sure we can come up with something," Frankie replied, just as seriously.

"Thank you very much," the father said. "You've made her day." He glanced down at his daughter. "Say goodbye now."

The little cowgirl threw her arms around Frankie. "Bwye, Fwankie."

Once again, a small pang twinged in Frankie's heart. "Bye, sweetheart."

The little girl took her father's hand and, with a final wave, melted into the crowd. The tug of longing still strong, she looked to find Luciano watching her, his expression unreadable.

Luciano's leg brushed against hers as the shuttlebus jostled them. Frankie rested her hand lightly on his thigh, marveling at the hard muscles she felt beneath his blue jeans.

"How are you feeling?" she said.

In a few minutes, they would enter the Thomas and Mack Arena for the last time before someone would be crowned this year's champion. The previous nine nights had flown by with Luciano consistently placing or winning. All he needed to do was finish in third place or better, and he would walk away with the gold buckle.

"Ready. Strangely calm but keyed up at the same time. Tonight could change everything." He rested his large hand on hers.

"Luc, no matter what, I am proud of you." Her eyes glowed with her love for him.

He smiled at her, the wrinkles she loved so much crinkling around his eyes. "I know, and I love you for that, but I will be disappointed in myself. I want this, Frankie. I want it so much I can almost taste it," he said fiercely.

The bus pulled to a halt, the whoosh of the door filling Frankie with nerves as she realized that, for her man, everything hinged on the next few hours. She reached up and gently touched his shoulder.

"Ready?"

"More than you will ever know." He stood calmly. As they walked down the steps of the bus, a sense of anticipation flowed from Luciano to her. There was nothing more for her to do but believe in him and be there for whatever the night would bring.

It was a moment slowed in time. The contorting bull, dust rising from his hooves as they pounded into the sand, the force vibrating through flesh, driven mad by the need to free himself from the spurring weight of the cowboy that sought to ride him. His sinuous hide, twisting about his muscular frame as both locked in a battle of wills to conquer the other. The cacophony of noise from the crowd faded away as Frankie leaned forward in her seat, her knuckles white as fingernails dug into denim-clad thighs, willing the clock to speed up. And then it was over, eight seconds flashing on the screen.

The crowd roared their approval as Gabi shrieked and jumped to her feet with Senhor Eduardo, hugging as they both celebrated. The crowd was jubilant, a deafening chorus of whooping and hollering, feet stamping and clapping. The excitement was palpable as it buzzed through the charged air.

Frankie let her breath out, watching as Luciano climbed to his feet. The bull was safely shunted out the gate as Joao and some other Brazilian riders rushed the arena, their national flags held aloft in jubilant hands. Luciano was hefted to their shoulders as they reveled in his achievement. He had done it. Luciano Navarro was the world champion.

The announcer finally made his way through the crush of madly celebrating Brazilians to Luciano. "Luciano Navarro, the world champion. How does it feel?"

"Amazing. This is something I have dreamed about since I was a little kid."

"You have had a great year and are our very deserving gold buckle winner. Are there some folks you would like to thank?"

Luciano took the mic from the announcer, his countrymen growing respectfully quiet. "My sponsors, especially Black Angus, Bryce, the PBR for the events, my friends here." He gestured to his countrymen. He was rewarded with a rousing cheer. "Eduardo, Joao. But there is someone else that all of this—*all* of this—I want to share with." He looked into the crowd. "Frankie? Querida, where are you?" The crowd twisted in their seats as they sought to find the mysterious Frankie.

Gabi nudged Frankie to her feet. "I'm here," she called, waving madly at him.

"Please, Frankie, come down here." She stood, an expectant hush surrounding her, at odds with the packed stadium. Her footsteps seemed loud as she made her way down the central stairs, an official meeting her halfway and ushering her onto the sand. She felt dwarfed as she nervously approached Luciano on the podium, the odor of livestock and sweat filling her nose. Luciano turned and spoke to Joao before the two men clasped hands.

Frankie watched, as if through tunnel vision, as he leapt to the arena floor, broad chaps flaring as he landed. Frankie admired the grace in his economical movements. Playful shadows cast by the arena light danced about his feet as he rushed toward her, lifting her off the ground in a giant bear hug. The fabric of his shirt was still damp from his perspiration as it whispered softly against her cheek when she snuggled into him.

"Querida, when I was little, all I wanted to be was world champion. I have it, but it is nothing if I don't have you to share it with. I love you, Frankie. I want to share everything I have, all that I am, with you."

He sunk down to one knee and opened his hand to reveal a little velvet box he had concealed there. He swallowed, his Adam's apple bobbing up and down, never taking his eyes from Frankie's. He opened it to reveal the gorgeous solitaire diamond ring within.

"Frankie, my heart, my Querida, will you marry me?"

Luciano's lovingly expectant face blurred in front of Frankie as tears shimmered in her eyes. She nodded as they cascaded down her face. "Yes, Luc, so much a yes, my love."

He let out a holler and jumped to his feet, his gaze locked with hers. The stadium erupted wildly around them, but they only had eyes for each other. Luciano gently took her face in his hands and slowly lowered his head.

"I love you, Frankie."

"I love you, too, Luc. Now, hurry up and kiss me," she commanded, her heart fluttering in her chest as her cowboy's lips finally met hers. Her cowboy, now and forever.

EPILOGUE

The makeup artist gave Frankie's lips a final flourish of color before stepping back to admire her handiwork. "He will not be able to take his eyes off you," she said.

Frankie got out of the makeup chair as her friends gathered round, a riot of giddy excitement as she held her kimono closed. "Well guys, I guess it's time to get me gussied up in the dress."

Deb walked over and reverently took the white dress down from its hanger and held it up, appraising the best strategy to get Frankie in it without causing havoc to hair, makeup, or destruction of delicate lace. She quirked her head to the side, chewing on her lip.

"I think if two of us hold it wide, you should be able to stand there in the dive position with your hands out and slip right in."

With the help of Gabi on the other side and Megan giving helpful little tugs, the dress finally fell into place, its graceful lace overlay draping gently over Frankie's body.

"Now it's just lacing you in and we have safely completed the dressing procedure," Deb declared before suddenly falling silent.

Frankie gave a concerned glance over her shoulder to find her friend chalky-faced and sweating. "Are you okay? I thought I was the one that was meant to be battling nerves today."

Deb's hand flew to her mouth and she gave an involuntary spasm. "Quick, move away from Frankie's dress if you're going to be sick," commanded Gabi, giving Frankie's hand a tug to move her safely away.

"I'm fine," Deb said shakily. "Just a tummy bug or something."

"Yeah, sure. That's what all the knocked-up ladies say," joked Megan.

Frankie watched as Deb's chalky complexion became, if possible, even paler. "Maybe you should sit down for a bit and have a drink of water."

She moved her veil and bouquet off a nearby sofa and Deb sunk gratefully down into its cushions, her eyes closed as she took deep breaths.

"Are you going to be okay? You look really crook." Megan began fanning her with a cushion.

"I'll be fine," muttered Deb. "Just give me a moment. It'll pass."

"Well, this might take your mind off it a bit," Gabi said. "I heard some gossip when I was at the petrol station."

"'Cause that's where all the good goss comes from," Megan said, giving her a wry look. "The servo."

"The servo? It doesn't matter. Anyway, apparently there's a new farrier in town. He specializes in working medical cases with the vets," Gabi said.

"Is the interesting part that he's cute?" asked Deb without opening her eyes.

"Well, for your information, he is apparently easy on the eyes, but that's not the interesting bit. He's an Aussie, so I thought maybe you might know him," she continued on, undeterred.

"'Cause Australia is such a small country after all," Frankie retorted.

"Well, for what it's worth, his name is Mitch. Mitch Eddison."

"Oh my gosh, Mitch has moved here?" Megan looked wide-eyed at Frankie. "How do you feel about that?"

"Like she cares. Look at her. She's standing here in her bloody wedding dress for Pete's sake," Deb said, a little more color in her cheeks.

Gabi looked around, slightly taken aback by the reaction the name she'd said had just caused. "So, you guys aren't happy he's here?"

"She's right, mate. He's just an old friend. It's a bit of a surprise, but it doesn't matter. Nothing matters today, except that I get to marry my Luciano." Frankie felt the rightness of her words. "Now, help me with this veil, and let's get this show on the road."

Frankie stood beneath the wildflower-covered arch, a perfect match to her bouquet made up of the same flowers as the first bunch Luciano had ever given her. A whisper of a breeze caressed the back of her neck, her hair tickling the sensitive skin.

She looked down the flower-strewn aisle to where the cowboy that held her heart stood, proud and tall, his back to her. She marveled at the threads of emotion he had wrapped around her, binding her to him in a rich tapestry of love. Joao stood beside him, eyes wide at the sight of her standing there, and leaned forward to whisper into Luciano's ear. He turned, his eyes glistening as he took in the vision before him. Their eyes met, and as the first strains of music filled the air, Frankie walked toward the man that held her heart.

Her cowgirl's dream.

THE END

As an Indie Author, reviews help me get my books noticed. If you enjoyed reading Frankie's story as much as I did writing it, please leave a review. It will make all the difference to me.

If you loved, *A Cowgirl's Dream* sign up for my newsletter to get exclusive chapters of Frankie and Luciano's wedding day—not to mention the mischief the girls get up to on the hen's party.

Now, turn the page as the Affinity Stud Ranch story continues with Deb...

*D*eb cautiously sipped the ginger beer, hopeful it would ease the nausea that threatened to storm her oesophagus and purge the contents of her stomach. It was getting beyond a joke. She hadn't managed to keep a full meal down for days now. At first, she put it down to the dodgy servo hotdog she had eaten, but now she was seriously starting to consider that she might have a medical condition on her hands.

There was only one thing left for a crook girl to do—consult Doctor Google. Typing in her symptoms, she took another careful sip. So far, so good. Okay, here we go, she thought as her screen filled with results. Anxiety, poor diet and dehydration, lupus, bowel cancer, irritable bowel syndrome. Geeze, she was seriously ill!

"Are you okay, Deb?" Frankie shifted uneasily in her chair. "You look a little queasy."

"Actually, she looks flat out like a lizard drinking," Megan griped. "When you're ready, dishes need to be done and it's your turn."

"Why is she giving a lizard a drink?" Gabi scrunched her

face up in confusion. "I didn't even know she had a pet lizard."

"It just means she's not that busy," Frankie explained. "I'll do the dishes before I head home. But I'm only doing it because you look awful, Deb. Aren't you feeling better yet?"

"I don't think I ever will, unless I can beat cancer," Deb muttered under her breath.

"What?" Frankie raised her chin in question.

"Never mind. Just talking to myself."

Megan perched herself on the arm of the sofa. "Guess who I saw this morning at the feed store?"

"Don't care, I'm dying here." Deb put her phone down as she accepted the inevitability of her prognosis.

"You're such a party pooper sometimes, Deb. But I'm going to ignore you." Megan stuck out her tongue. "I saw Mitch. And that's not all. I invited him to see the ranch tomorrow."

Frankie dried her hands on a towel. "I'm going to leave these dishes to drain and head home. Luciano will be home soon, and I don't want him getting lonely, if you know what I mean." Frankie winked smugly at the girls.

Deb thought she looked disgustingly happy. A wave of nausea forced her to close her eyes as she battled through it. Opening her eyes again once it passed, she locked them squarely with her friend. "Awesome, Megan," she said sarcastically. "Just awesome. And now, if you'll excuse me, I'm going to be sick."

Deb's story, A *Cowgirl's Heart*, is available for purchase on Amazon or free on Kindle Unlimited

ACKNOWLEDGMENTS

A debt of gratitude to my editor Rebekah Groves for her patience with me.

Another big thanks to Megan from Designed with Grace for her cover design. Who knew it was so hard to get pictures of hot cowboys that were wearing shirts.

A fiery cowgirl with big dreams. A movie star far from home. When their two worlds collide, will their love be strong enough to hold them together or will they be pulled apart

A cowgirl's billionaire

Release Dec 2020

Christmas Standalone Books

Boots and Mistletoe

Edith MacKenzie or Eddie Mac to her friends is an author of sweet and wholesome contemporary cowboy romance. They say in literary circles to write what you know, and Eddie has certainly taken that to heart. Before embarking on a writing career, she trained horses professionally and brings that wealth of knowledge to her writing.

Now a mum to a boy and girl, as well as wife, she delights with her tales of strong cowgirls and their adventures in finding love. When not weaving the love stories of her characters, she enjoys hanging out with her family and animals, as well as reading, fishing and camping.

Just remember—once a cowgirl, always a cowgirl.

facebook.com/EddieMacAuthor
instagram.com/edith_mackenzie_author
amazon.com/Edith-MacKenzie
bookbub.com/profile/edith-mackenzie

GLOSSARY OF AUSSIE SLANG

Now everyone knows that cobbers from the Land Down Under speak the Queen's English, but if you don't know to Tracky Daks from your Servo, I've put together a quick little cheat sheet.

A few kangaroos loose in the top paddock - To not be working with all of your mental capacity, to be a bit daft

A few stubbies short of a six pack - Crazy

Ankle Bitter - Small child

Arvo - Afternoon

Aussie Salute - wave flies away

Bail - to cancel plans

Belly Up - Go out of business

Blind - Intoxicated

Bloody - Very. Used to extenuate a point

Bloody oath - Yes or its true

Bludger - Someone who is lazy

Buggered - Exhausted

Buggie Smugglers - Speedos, swimming trunks

Cactus - Die

Can't be bothered - Not in a mood to do anything

Cark it - Die

Choccy Bikkie - Chocolate cookie

Clucky - Feeling maternal

Crook - Feeling sick

Daks - Trousers e.g. Tracky Daks are tracksuit pants

Dog's breakfast - Messy (does not relate to food), a bit of a shambles

Dry as a dead dingo's doing - Exceptionally dry

Fair Go - Give someone a chance

Flat out like a lizard drinking' - Not doing very much at all

Going off like a frog in a blender - Going off by itself can be good e.g. the surf was going off - it was good surf conditions.

If Going off is added to anything else it is bad, in this case you can imagine what a frog in a blender would feel like

Good on ya - Good for you (sarcastic)

Go Troppo - To lose the plot, go crazy

Grog - Alcohol

Have a barney - To have a tiff or blue

Hit the frog and toad - Hit the road, get going

Idiot Box - TV

Jumper - Sweater

Man's not a camel - A man gets thirsty and would indeed like the beverage you are offering him

Mate - Friend or conversely could be someone you barely know

Mate's Rates - To get a large discount because you are friends

Nay, Yeah - Yes

Pull the wool over someone's eyes - To trick or mislead someone

Reckon - For sure

Ripsnorter - Can also be interchanged with beaut, bonza. Someone doing something exceptionally good

Servo - Petrol Station

Shout - To pay for the next round of drinks

Six one way, half a dozen the other - Undecided

Sparrow Fart - Before the crack of dawn. Very, very early in the morning

Spit the dummy - To throw a tantrum. A similar display of when an infant spits out their pacifier "dummy" and bursts into a hysterical crying fit.

Stone the flamin' crow - An utterance of surprise of annoyance

Struth - God's truth. Used to express surprise or dismay

She'll be right - Everything is going to okay

Tell 'em they're dreaming - Is never in a million years going to happen

Tighter than a fish's bum - Said person is very frugal with their money

To blow smoke up someone's bum - To give praise that might make the other person cocky or overly confident

Two Pot Screamer - Someone that is a cheap drunk and can not hold their alcohol very well

Up yourself - Stuck up

Ute - Pickup Truck

Whinge - Complain

Whoop whoop - Middle of nowhere

Wrap ya laughing gear 'round that - Eat this

Yarn - To talk or tell tall tales

Yeah, nay - No

You bloody ripper - Very good, a job well done

Made in the USA
Monee, IL
20 June 2021